THE USBORNE BOOK OF

GAMES

AND

PUZZLES

THE USBORNE BOOK OF
GAMES
AND
PUZZLES

Edited by Alastair Smith
Designed by Fiona Brown

Material in this book originally developed by
Jane Bingham, Kim Blundell, Karen Bryant-Mole,
Moira Butterfield, Anne Civardi, Robyn Gee,
Ray Gibson, Susannah Leigh, Peter McClelland,
Lisa Miles, Tony Potter, Jenny Tyler

Illustrated by
Simone Abel, Iain Ashman, Kim Blundell,
Malcolm English, Peter Geissler, Brenda Haw,
Colin King, Chris Lyon, Graham Round

First published in 1994 by Usborne Publishing Ltd, Usborne House, 83-85 Saffron Hill, London, EC1N 8RT, England.
Copyright © Usborne Publishing Ltd, 1994.
The name Usborne and the device ⬙ are Trade Marks of Usborne Publishing Ltd.
Printed in Great Britain.
UE First published in America March 1995.

Contents

GAMES TO MAKE

You can make these games using pieces of junk, such as cardboard, paper plates and yogurt containers. You'll need a good supply of adhesive tape and glue to put them together. Some of the games are fun to play alone. Others are perfect for two or more players.

The answers to the BRAIN CRUNCHER questions can be found on page 96.

Eggs on a plate

This is a game for two players. Before you can play it, you will need to make six egg shapes out of pieces of cardboard, along with a spinning pointer device and a couple of pictures of chickens drawn onto paper plates.

You will need

- Two large paper plates • Small paper plate
- Strip of thin cardboard 10 x 2cm (4 x 1in)
- Scissors • Ball-point pen • Paper fastener
- 24 pieces of thin cardboard
4 x 5cm (1½ x 2in) • Felt-tip pens

Making the pointer

 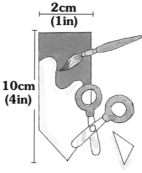 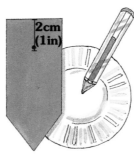 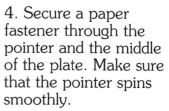 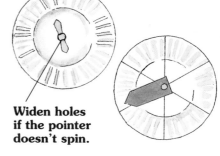

Widen holes if the pointer doesn't spin.

1. Turn over a large paper plate and divide it into six sections. Write "egg on" and "egg off" in alternate spaces.

2. Cut a piece of thin cardboard and trim one end to a point. Decorate it with a red felt-tip, or using red paint.

3. Using a ball-point pen poke a hole in the middle of the plate, and a hole in the pointer 2cm (1in) from its straight end.

4. Secure a paper fastener through the pointer and the middle of the plate. Make sure that the pointer spins smoothly.

Making eggs

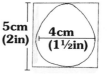

Draw egg shapes onto the 24 small pieces of thin cardboard as shown above. Then cut out the shapes. You could decorate them with pieces of wrapping paper.

Egg-making tips

• Draw and cut out one egg and use the shape to draw the others.

• Instead of decorating the eggs, you could cut 12 from white paper and 12 from brown paper.

To decorate the plates you could copy or trace the chickens shown on these pages. Decorate them brightly (felt-tips are best for this). Alternatively, you could draw on bird designs of your own, such as geese, ducks or turkeys.

These chickens are drawn in a comic style, but you could make yours more realistic if you like.

Tasty idea

Instead of using home-made eggs you could use pieces of chocolate or chocolate eggs. At the end of the game you could eat the eggs that you have on your plate.

BRAIN CRUNCHER

If yesterday's tomorrow was Thursday, what day is the day after tomorrow's yesterday?

How to play

Each player chooses a chicken plate, then takes 12 eggs. Put six eggs on your plate and leave six off. Then take turns closing your eyes and spinning the pointer with your finger. Move eggs on or off your plate according to where the pointer stops. The game ends when one of you has collected 12 eggs on a plate, or a plate is empty. The player with most eggs wins. You could shorten the game by setting a time limit.

Extra idea

Write "forfeit" in one section on the spinner plate. If you make the pointer stop in this section, your opponent can choose a forfeit for you to do, such as singing a song or imitating a chicken.

Cannonboard

To play this game you fire marbles from a tube and try to score points by getting them to land in little cups. You can play this game on your own or you could hold a competition with your friends.

Making the board

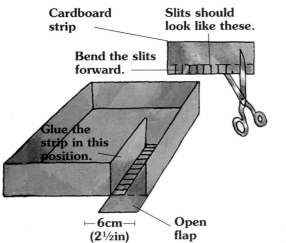

Cardboard strip

Slits should look like these.

Bend the slits forward.

Glue the strip in this position.

⊢6cm⊣ (2½in)

Open flap

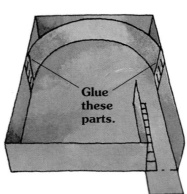

Glue these parts.

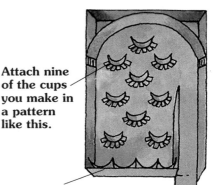

Attach nine of the cups you make in a pattern like this.

Attach four cups here.

1. Cut a flap in one corner of the box. Then cut a strip of cardboard that is half the length of the box and as high. Cut lots of slits on one side of the strip. Then glue the strip to the box.

2. Cut a strip of cardboard about 1½ times the width of the box. Cut slits at both ends. Bend the strip smoothly, then glue the ends of the strip to the sides of the box.

3. Cut 13 pieces of cardboard so that they are about 8cm (3in) long and 3cm (1in) wide. Cut slits at one edge of each piece. Bend back the slits and then bend each piece to form cups.

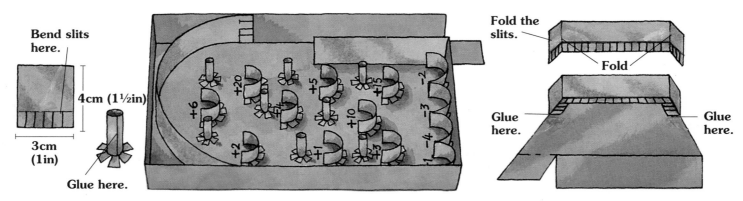

Bend slits here.

4cm (1½in)

3cm (1in)

Glue here.

Fold the slits.

Fold

Glue here.

Glue here.

Turn the box upside down.

4. Cut out eight strips of cardboard. Cut slits along the edge of each strip. Roll the strips into little tubes, then glue the edges together. Finally, bend back the slits.

5. Glue the tubes onto the box, as shown above, to form barriers, which will make the game more challenging to play. Draw or paint the point values inside each cup.

6. Cut some cardboard about 50cm (20in) wide and about 6cm (2½in) high. Cut slits along its edge. Fold the strip about 8cm (3in) from either end. Glue it under the back of the box.

The cannon

Make holes in the circles.

The adhesive tape wrapping should look like this.

Loop through.

1. Draw two circles on some cardboard, using the end of the cardboard tube. Cut them out so that they are 0.5cm (¼in) smaller than the tube's end. Glue the two circles together.

2. Push the end of a pencil through the hole in the cardboard circles. Tape the circles onto the pencil very firmly, in a similar way to the one in the picture above.

3. Link four strong elastic bands together, as shown in the picture above. Then make a hole in either side of the tube, about 3cm (1in) from one of the ends.

Tie a knot here.   **Tie a knot here.**

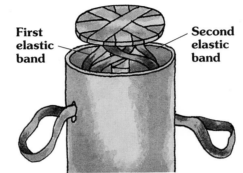

First elastic band   **Second elastic band**

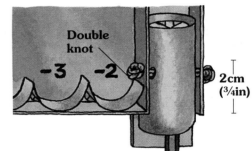

Double knot −3 −2   **2cm (¾in)**

4. Thread the elastic bands through the holes in the cardboard tube, so that the ends are sticking out of its side. Knot the ends very loosely.

5. Push the cardboard disk and the pencil up the tube. First slip one elastic band over the disk and then the other. Untie the loose knots.

6. Make a hole half way up the two pieces of cardboard, about 2cm (¾in) from the open flap on the box. Push the elastic band ends through the holes, as shown above. Then tie a double knot in each end.

How to play

To play cannonboard, fire the marbles out of the cannon and try to get them into the cups with the highest point values.

To fire a marble, put one into the top of the cannon. Pull back the pencil and then let it go.

Allow each player to have four rounds, with five shots per round. At the end of each round add up the scores for each player. The player with the highest score is the winner.

Blow soccer

Blow soccer is such fun to play that it is worth taking the time to make the game. Instead of a ball you use dried peas. Using all of your spare breath you blow through a drinking straw to direct the peas into your opponent's goal.

You will need
• Cardboard box at least 30 x 45cm (12 x 18in) • Green paint
• Paintbrush • Ruler • Felt-tip pen
• Mug • 2 drinking straws • Scissors
• Handful of dried peas • Bread knife
• Yogurt container • Adhesive tape

Making the stadium

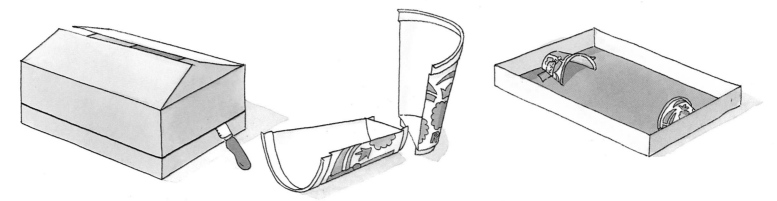

1. Cut around the box with the bread knife, about 6cm (2½in) from the bottom. Be careful when you do this, or ask a grown up to do it for you.

2. Cut a yogurt container in half, as shown in the picture above, using scissors or a bread knife. You'll use these to make the goals for the soccer field.

3. Paint the playing area green, so that it looks like grass. Then tape the halved yogurt containers onto the middle of both ends of the field.

Excited soccer fans add to the atmosphere of a big game.

The person who scores the most goals is the winner. You could choose sides, and pretend that you are replaying a famous match.

4. Draw a line across the middle of the field. Draw around a mug to make a circle around the middle of the line. Then draw fans around the edge of the playing area.

How to play

Put ten dried peas into the circle. Before you start, you and your opponent should position yourselves at either end of the field, ready to blow through your drinking straws.

When you're ready, blow through your straw very hard. Blow the peas into the opposite goal. The game ends when all peas are in the goals. The scorer of the most goals wins.

Buzzing bees

To make this game you will need to make one flower for each person who wants to play. The more players there are, the more exciting and fun the game is.

You will need
- Large squares of decorative paper
- Glue • Scissors • Pencil
- Small plate 15cm (6in) across
- Adhesive tape • Music

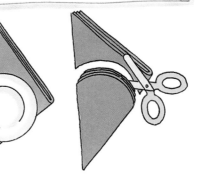

1. Fold a large square of paper in half across the middle, as indicated above, so that the top will fold over to meet the bottom.

2. When the paper is in half, fold it in half again, this time from left to right. Then fold it in half again, this time diagonally, as shown.

3. Place a small plate on top of the folded paper. Draw around the curve as shown and cut along the line. Open out the paper. The paper will be shaped like a flower.

How to play

One person controls the music, while the others dance. When the controller chooses, he or she stops the music. The dancers must buzz to a flower. When the music starts again, the music controller removes a flower. The next time the music stops one player will be left out. Keep doing this until only one person remains. The last person left is the winner.

To make the middle of a flower, draw around a small plate and cut out the shape. Then glue the shape to the flower.

Tips for playing the game

When you play, take off your shoes so that you don't break any of the flowers.

Music played on a tape player is best for this game as it is easily controlled.

Tape the flowers to the floor, so that they don't get kicked around during the game.

Cops and robbers

This game is for two people. One plays as the cops and the other plays as the robbers. Use your characters to trap your opponent's and capture them. To capture them, you have to use a special trapping device, which is shown below. The full rules are explained on the opposite page.

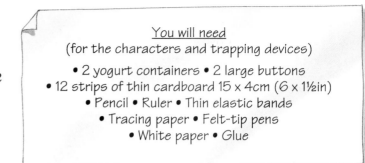

Making the characters

1. Take the strips of cardboard. Fold them in half and bend out the ends. Then glue the two halves together. The two bent-out ends should form a stand.

2. Using tracing paper, trace the cop pattern onto six of the cardboard pieces you have just made. Trace six robbers onto the other cardboard pieces.*

3. When you have drawn the cops and robbers, decorate their clothes. You could dress them in old-fashioned clothes, like the ones shown above.

Making the trapping devices

To use the device, pull up the button and then let it go sharply. The button will make a sharp clapping sound.

Make a hole, 1cm (½in) from the base, on either side of the yogurt containers. Thread thin elastic through the holes and thread a big button onto the elastic. Tie knots in the ends.

Draw a picture of a cop's head on a piece of paper and a robber's head on another piece. Then glue one onto one of the trapping devices, and the other onto the other device.

* **There is a guide to tracing on page 96.**

Making the board

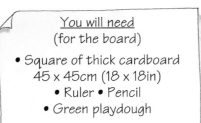

You will need
(for the board)

- Square of thick cardboard
  45 x 45cm (18 x 18in)
  - Ruler • Pencil
- Green playdough

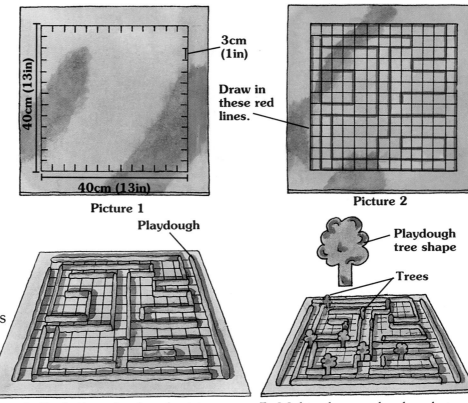

Picture 1

40cm (13in)

40cm (13in)

3cm (1in)

Draw in these red lines.

Picture 2

1. Draw a square 40 x 40cm (13 x 13in). Then draw marks every 3cm (1in) along the four sides of the square, as shown in picture 1.

2. Rule lines from the top marks to the bottom marks and from side to side to make small squares. Draw in the red lines as shown in picture 2.

Playdough

3. To make hedges, roll pieces of playdough into long strips, each about 0.5cm (¼in) thick. Put the strips along the red lines drawn on the cardboard.

4. Push the playdough strips down gently so that they stick to the cardboard. Then pinch the strips until they are about 1cm (½in) high.

Playdough tree shape

Trees

5. Make eleven playdough tree shapes. Put them on top of the hedges. Check the big picture below to ensure that you've put the trees in the right places.

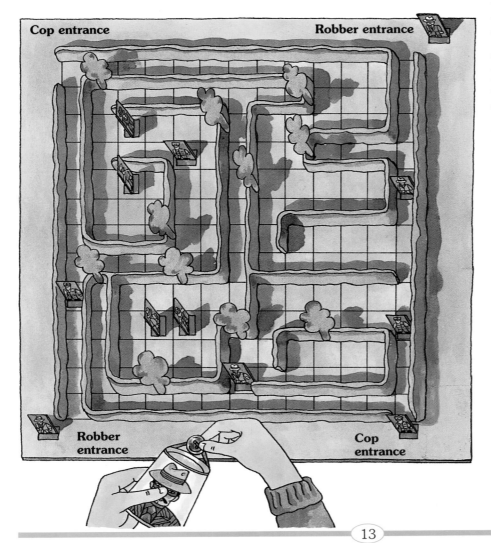

Cop entrance

Robber entrance

Robber entrance

Cop entrance

How to play

The idea is to capture all of your opponent's characters. One player moves the cops. The other moves the robbers.

To start, put three cops at each cop entrance and three robbers at each robber entrance. Each player moves one of their pieces five squares in a turn. Pieces can be moved in any direction, except diagonally.

To capture an enemy, your piece must land on a square next to one occupied by an enemy. To make the capture, take your trapping device, pull the button, then let go of it to fire. The enemy is then removed. If you forget to use the trapping device, your capture is not complete and your opponent's piece must be allowed to escape.

Pieces cannot jump hedges, or make a capture through them, unless they are next to a tree. The winner is the player who captures all enemy pieces.

Flick snooker

This game is based on snooker. To play it, you try to flick thick counters off one another into pockets in the corners of your snooker table. Flicking the counters can bruise your finger, so it's best to guard it with a strip of cardboard strapped on using adhesive tape.

You will need

- A cardboard box 72 x 50cm (30 x 20in)
- Thin cardboard • 4 old socks
- 21 draughts/checkers counters (10 of each of two different shades, plus one of another shade)
- Small yogurt container • Adhesive tape
- Strong glue • Scissors • Pencil

How to make the game

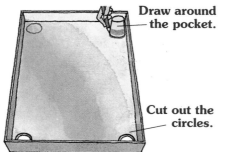

Draw around the pocket.

Cut out the circles.

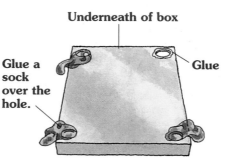

Underneath of box

Glue a sock over the hole.

Glue

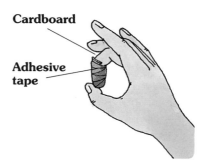

Cardboard

Adhesive tape

1. Draw a circle in each corner on the inside of the box, using a small yogurt container as a guide. Cut out the four circles using a pair of sharp scissors.

2. To make the corner pockets, cut the feet off four old socks. Glue one foot over each hole on the underneath of the box, as shown above.

3. To make a finger guard, cut a strip of thin cardboard. Put it over the nail of your third finger. Wrap tape around it, to hold the guard in place.

How to play

One player uses one shade of counters, such as black, and the other uses the other shade, such as red. Decide who's going to start.

The object of the game is to get all of your opponent's counters into the pockets, by flicking one of yours against one of theirs.

If you get a counter into a pocket, have another turn. Keep going until you fail to get one of your opponent's counters into a pocket.

If you flick the "bonus counter" into a pocket, pick one of your counters out of a pocket and put it back on the board. Also, put the bonus counter back on the board.

The winner is the first person to flick all of their opponent's counters into the pockets.

To start the game, set the counters as shown in this picture.

You might like to raise your playing board by putting a pile of books under each corner.

Bonus counter

Table tennis

For this game you'll need to use a table. If you don't have a table tennis ball, you could make your own by wrapping a small ball of paper tightly with adhesive tape.

You will need
- Thick cardboard 48 x 20cm (18 x 8in)
- Thin cardboard 20 x 20cm (8 x 8in)
- Sheet of sponge 48 x 20cm (18 x 8in)
- Small plate 15cm (6in) across • String
- Old nylon stocking • Adhesive tape
- Table tennis ball (or some sheets of paper)

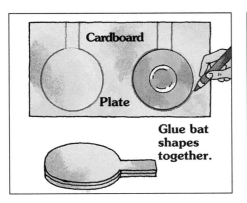

1. Rule four lines, 4cm (1½in) apart and 10cm (4in) long, on thick cardboard. Draw a circle around a small plate at the bottom of the lines. Cut out the shapes. Glue them together.

2. Using the same plate, draw four circles on a sheet of thin sponge, as shown above. Cut out around the larger circles. Then glue them to both sides of the cardboard bats.

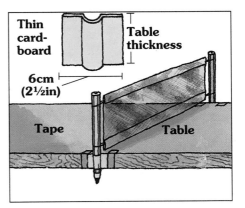

3. Wrap string tightly around the handles. Glue the ends and wrap adhesive tape around them. Push a pencil up each of the handles, to make them stronger.

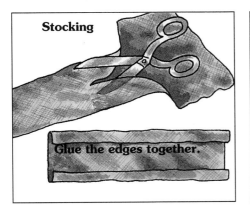

4. To make the net, cut the foot off an old stocking. Then cut it open. Fold it over and put glue along it, about 2cm (1in) in from both edges.

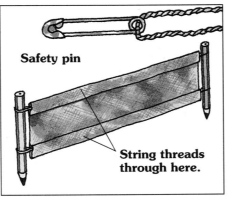

5. Cut two bits of string 80cm (30in) long. Loop each through a closed safety pin. Thread them through the stocking. Tie the ends to two pencils.

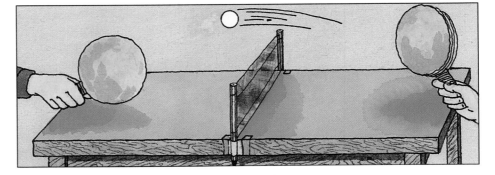

6. Tape two pieces of thin cardboard to the middle of each side of the table. Push the pencils into the cardboard shapes so that they stand up.

How to play

The aim is to be the first to score 21 points. You score a point when the other player fails to return your shot.

Flip a coin to see who serves first. Whoever wins serves five serves in a row. Then the other player takes five serves, and so on, until the end of the game.

You must win by at least two clear points.

When you serve, the ball must bounce on both sides of the net before your opponent hits it.

However, the ball must not bounce on your side when you return a shot.

Fishing game

For this game you need at least two players. However, you could have lots of players, provided you can make enough fishing rods for them to use and enough fish for them to catch. You'll need little magnets to put on each player's fishing rod, so that it can pick up the fish.

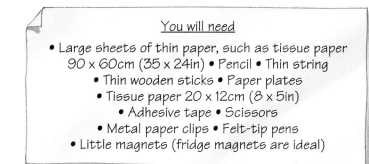

You will need
- Large sheets of thin paper, such as tissue paper 90 x 60cm (35 x 24in) • Pencil • Thin string
- Thin wooden sticks • Paper plates
- Tissue paper 20 x 12cm (8 x 5in)
- Adhesive tape • Scissors
- Metal paper clips • Felt-tip pens
- Little magnets (fridge magnets are ideal)

Making the fish

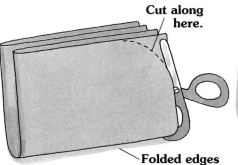

Cut along here.

Folded edges

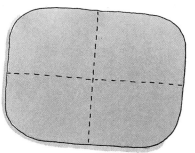

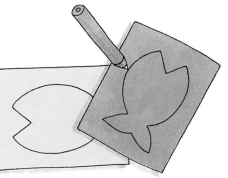

1. Fold a large sheet of blue tissue paper into four. Make the outer corners round, as shown.

2. Open it and lay it flat on the floor. When you play the game, this will be your pond.

3. On pieces of tissue paper and wrapping paper draw simple fish shapes about 15cm (6in) long. You will need to make 15 to 20 fish.

Fishy tips
- Use thin wrapping paper or the magnet won't pick up the fish.
- Cut out a number of fish at a time by cutting through several layers of paper.
- Adjust the rod according to your height by winding or unwinding the string around the stick.
- To store the game wind the string around each stick and fold the pond. Keep all the pieces in a box.

4. Cut out the shapes neatly, using scissors. After, you could decorate them using eye-catching felt-tip pens, so that they look like tropical fish.

5. Turn the fish shapes over. Place a paper clip near the mouth of each fish. Then secure the paper clips with adhesive tape.

Racing fish game

Cut out large tissue paper fish shapes about 25cm (10in) long. Race your fish by blowing them or flapping them with rolled-up newspaper.

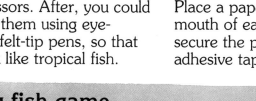

Making the fishing rod

To make a fishing rod, tie one end of a piece of string around a magnetic shape. Secure it by tying a knot in the string.

Tie the other end of the string onto the end of a stick. Use adhesive tape to prevent the string from slipping.

Stick

You might like to make a trophy out of cardboard, covered with tin foil. You could award it to the winner.

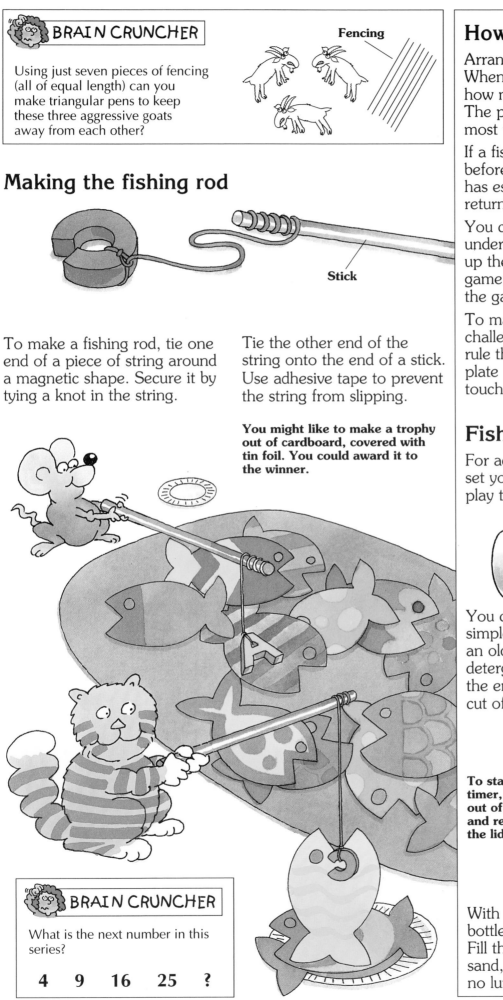

How to play

Arrange the fish on the pond. When the signal is given, see how many fish you can catch. The player who catches the most fish is the winner.

If a fish falls off a fishing rod before it reaches a plate then it has escaped and should be returned to the pond.

You could write a score on the underside of each fish and add up the scores at the end of the game. The highest scorer wins the game.

To make the game more challenging, you could make a rule that fish must land on a plate without your hands touching the fish.

Fishing timer

For added excitement, you could set yourself a time limit when you play this game.

You can make a simple timer using an old dishwashing detergent bottle. First, cut the empty bottle in half. Then cut off the tip and close the lid.

To start the timer, take it out of the jar and remove the lid.

When the salt or sand has run out, your time is up.

With the lid closed, balance the bottle upside down in a glass jar. Fill the bottle with salt or dry sand, making sure that there are no lumps in it.

Mouse trap

Mouse trap is a game that tests the speed of your reactions. To play, you will need at least three people. In the game one person must act as the trapper, trying to catch the mice, which are being held by the other players. Take turns to be the trapper.

Making the mice

1. Decorate the corks so that they look different from one another. Then make a hole through the middle of each one, using closed scissors or a knitting needle, as shown above.

2. Loop string, about 40cm (16in) long, around a hair clip. Then push it through the hole in a cork and double-knot the end of the string. Do the same to all of the corks.

3. To make the mouse ears, cut out two pieces of cloth in the shapes shown above. Glue two of them to the top of each cork. When the ears are dry your mouse is ready to use.

Making the spinner

Trace* the pattern shown on the right onto some thin cardboard. Rule lines from corner to corner, as shown. Cut the shape out very carefully. Paint the triangles and write on the numbers. Sharpen a used match or toothpick with a pencil sharpener. Push it through the middle of the spinner, where all the lines meet.

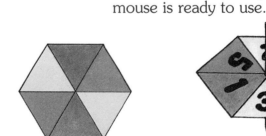

Pattern for spinner

Toothpick or sharpened matchstick

How to play

The holders put their mice on the cardboard circle and hold their tails. The trapper spins the spinner. When it stops on a 6 or 4 the trapper tries to trap mice under the container. The holders try to pull them away before being trapped.

The trapper scores 5 points for catching a mouse. A holder scores 5 points if he or she pulls the mouse before being caught by the trapper.

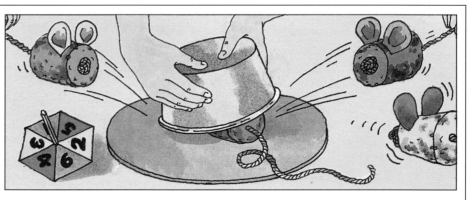

The winner is the person who has the most points after an agreed number of rounds – ten rounds, for example.

A holder loses 5 points if he or she pulls the mouse away when the spinner stops on a number other than a 6 or a 4.

* There is a guide to tracing on page 96.

Push and shove

This game tests how accurate your aim is. Either two players can play against each other, or four can play, in teams of two.

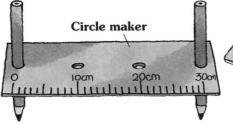

Circle maker

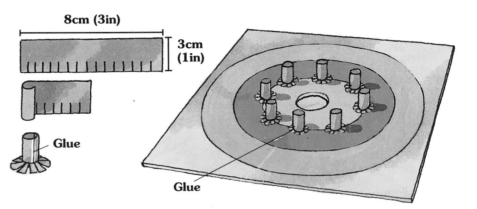

Middle of board

1. To make a circle maker measure out a piece of thick cardboard 30cm (12in) long. Punch holes in it at both ends and 10cm (4in) from both ends.

2. Find the middle of the square sheet of cardboard. Draw three circles, as shown above, using the holes in the circle maker.

Cut out hole.

Glue cardboard underneath.

8cm (3in)

3cm (1in)

Glue

Glue

3. Cut a hole, bigger than one of the counters, out of the middle of the board. Glue a square of cardboard underneath the hole. Then decorate the circles in a variety of shades.

4. Cut out eight pieces of cardboard, each about 8 x 3cm (3 x 1in). Make cuts along one edge of each piece. Roll them into posts. Glue the ends and bend out the cuts.

5. Glue the posts, at equal distances around the edge of the inside circle. The space between two posts should be big enough for the counters to go through.

How to play

If two people play, each has ten counters. If four play, each has five. Partners use the same shade of counters and sit opposite each other.

Take turns flicking the counters, one by one. Try to get them on to the high scoring circles. If a counter lands on a line, count the lower score. Try to flick them behind posts to avoid being hit. The player or team with the highest score after all 20 counters have been flicked is the winner.

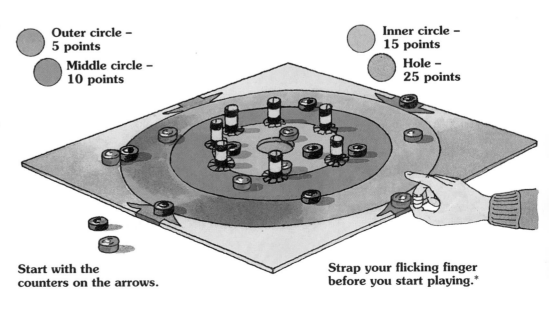

Outer circle – 5 points

Middle circle – 10 points

Inner circle – 15 points

Hole – 25 points

Start with the counters on the arrows.

Strap your flicking finger before you start playing.*

* For details on strapping and flicking your finger, see page 14.

Steady hand game

Using an old box, some wire, a battery and a tiny electrical buzzer you can make a game which really tests your control over your hands. You might have to buy some of the things for this game from a hardware shop, but they are not expensive.

Making the game

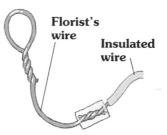

Florist's wire

Insulated wire

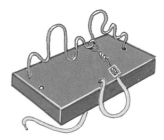

1. With a ball-point pen, make three holes in the lid of the shoe box as shown. Carefully strip 2.5cm (1in) of the covering off each end of the insulated wire.

2. Cut 15cm (6in) off the florist's wire and bend one end into a loop. Twist the other end onto a bare end of the insulated wire, then tape them together.

3. Feed the other end of the insulated wire through the middle hole in the lid. Bend the rest of the florist's wire to make a wiggly line. Thread the loop onto it.

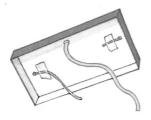

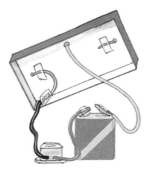

4. Push the ends of the wiggly wire through the holes at the ends of the shoe box lid. Tape both ends to the lid, leaving 10cm (4in) of one end hanging free.

5. Twist together the long end of the wiggly wire and the free buzzer wire. Tape the bare end of the insulated wire to the free battery terminal. The buzzer may sound.

How to play

Start with the loop at one end of the wiggly wire. Then, holding the looped wire in one hand, try to get it to the other end of the wiggly wire without letting the two pieces of wire touch.

If the wire loop and the wiggly wire touch, they will make an electrical connection which will cause the buzzer to sound.

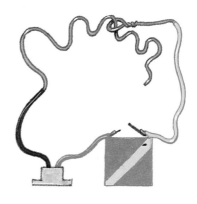

If the buzzer doesn't sound when the wires touch, check for any loose connections. If there are no loose connections, check that your battery has not run down.

6. Put the battery and buzzer in the box and put on the lid. Wind a little tape around the ends of the wiggly wire. You may need to bend the wire more so that it stands up better. Now try the game.

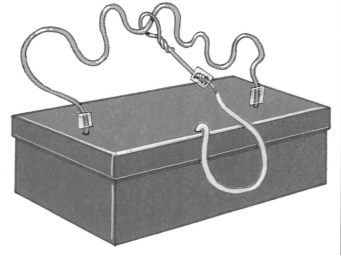

PICTURE PUZZLES

In this section there are seven intriguing scenes, containing things for you to spot. Before you answer the questions, read the story and look at the picture closely. Each puzzle will test your power of observation, so you'll have to be eagle-eyed to answer them correctly. You will find the correct solutions on pages 88-90.

The answers to the BRAIN CRUNCHERS can be found on page 96.

Planet puzzle

Archie the Astronaut and his robot dog have crashed on Puzzle Planet. They have never visited the planet before so they can't be sure whether they are safe.

Luckily, their *Outer Space Guidebook* explains how to recognize which parts of Puzzle Planet are safe and friendly and which are full of danger. A page from their guidebook is shown on the right.

Looking at their surroundings, can you tell what type of place they are in?

BRAIN CRUNCHER

You have a bag of cookies. You give half to your friend. Then you lose half of the cookies that you had left. Now you only have six cookies. How many did you have to start with?

The wizard's den

Wizard Wilf's Den

it's secret

Deep in the dungeon of a dark and dusty castle lies Wizard Wilf's secret den. Wilf spends his days mixing magic potions in his enormous cauldron, or brewing samples of tasty grog, which he shares with his friends. Today, Sorcerer Sophie is visiting him.

Unfortunately, the grog that Wilf made last week went wrong. The friends who drank it all turned into animals.

From the picture below, can you see how many of Wilf's friends drank the grog?

BRAIN CRUNCHER

Using this piece of
string, wrapped
around these
nine pegs, how
can you make
six squares?
The first has
been done
for you.

Sorcerer Sophie has come to see if a potion that she
ordered last week is ready. If it works it will make her
invisible. "I think it's ready," cries Wilf excitedly. "I'll just
test it to see if it works."

Wilf waves his magic wand. Suddenly there's a purple
flash and a puff of smoke. When it clears they see that
Sophie is still there, but lots of other things have vanished.

**Ten things have disappeared. Can you spot
them all?**

After the potion

Party trail

Pete the Pixie, who lives in Puzzle Town, has decided to have a party. He's sent an invitation to Katy and Tim, two of his best friends.

In the invitation Pete has asked Katy and Tim to stop at some shops to pick up things which will help make the party a roaring success. The invitation is shown below.

Can you spot which shops in town Katy and Tim must go to?

Can you see what is unusual about the flower shop?

Dear Katy and Tim,
Before you come to my party, here are a few things that I'd like you to do.

Love,
Pete the Pixie
xx

Buy some cakes for the party.

Get some party hats.

Buy some juicy fruit.

Get some dancing shoes.

Send the letters that I enclosed with this invitation.

MY BALLOONS! THEY'VE BEEN STOLEN!

A thief has stolen all the balloons in town. He's hiding somewhere. **Can you find him?**

BRAIN CRUNCHER

Pretend that you have seven pockets in your clothes. If you put one grape in the first pocket, two in the second, four in the third, and so on, doubling the number for each pocket, how many grapes will you have in all?

Goats on the loose

While walking on Puzzle Mountain, Poppy Pickaxe and her puppy Bernard come across Gretel the goatherd. Gretel is sobbing her heart out.

"Oh Poppy," she wails, "the music from some musicians down the hill has frightened all of my goats away. I've lost all seven of them. Can you see them? They are all brown with white faces."

Can you find Gretel's seven lost goats?

Gretel has also lost one of her ice skates. **Can you see it?**

Not including the goats, how many horned creatures are there in this scene?

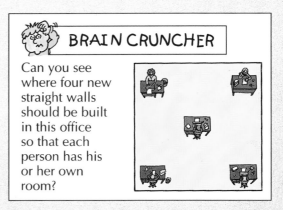

BRAIN CRUNCHER

Can you see where four new straight walls should be built in this office so that each person has his or her own room?

ZZZZZZ

Giant snails

Archie the Astronaut is looking around Puzzle Planet with his robot dog and two companions. He's come across some giant snails which seem to be attacking their friend, Victor the Vargon.

"These creatures are hungry!" cries Victor.

"It's OK," yells Archie, "these snails like eating blue space bananas best, and we can see seven, one for each of them!"

Can you see all seven blue bananas?

BRAIN CRUNCHER

Without drawing the shapes, can you tell how many spaces there are between the spokes of an eight-spoked wheel?

DON'T WORRY!

Puzzlesville garage

Mechanic Molly's garage is a mess. While trying to fix a customer's car she dropped her tools all over the floor. Now she can't find any of them. Her friends Katy and Tim have called in and are helping her to find them.

"I've lost a screwdriver, a saw, a hammer, a flashlight, a very big nail and my red cleaning cloth," moans Molly.

Katy and Tim look around the messy garage. It certainly isn't going to be an easy job.

Can you find Molly's lost tools?

Including Daisy, the dog mechanic, there are twelve animals in this picture. **Can you spot them all?**

BRAIN CRUNCHER

A car going at 30kmph (20mph) takes three minutes to reach the top of a hill. It takes three minutes at twice the speed to reach the bottom of the other side. How far has it gone when it reaches the bottom?

Ski lift

The Puzzle Town Tours company has organized a trip to the snowy mountain resort at Puzzle Mountain.

Eight people from the Puzzle Town party are trying to get on the ski lift, but they are having problems.

"This notice has really confused us. Which chairs should we use?" asks Roger Round.

Using the sign to help you, can you decide which skier should use which chair?

How many hats can you see in this picture?

BRAIN CRUNCHER

Town A is 30km (20 miles) from town B by mountain road and 15km (10 miles) using a tunnel. Cars must wait in line for 10 minutes before they can get into the tunnel. Which is the faster route by car, driving at 60kmph (40mph)?

Please read the instructions before taking the lift:

BLUE CHAIR - two adults only

RED CHAIR - one very tall person only

GREEN CHAIR - two adults with hats only

YELLOW CHAIR - cannot hold much weight

PURPLE CHAIR - two children only

RESTAURANT

WE ALWAYS TRAVEL TOGETHER.

Can you spot...?

On this page there are 19 things that have been shown throughout this section of the book. **Can you find where on the last 14 pages these things appear?** As a clue, there are three things on every double page picture. Beware, though, some of them appear in more than one of the scenes.

Ghost

Half-eaten cookie

Goofy cat

Motorcycle and sidecar

Bread tree

Crazy snake

Yellow mushroom

Ski pole

Yellow fruit

Juggling ball

Eggs in a nest

Snowman destroyer

Blue creature

Fish sign

Giant pink marshmallow

Space car

Mystery box

Bird of prey

Red-edged cloak

Spell the word ... backwards

BOARD GAMES

The following section contains games that you can play using the opened-out pages as your boards. You may need to use counters or a dice for some of them. Hold the pages flat by weighting the edges down with heavy things, such as a couple of books.

Before you start playing a game, make sure that you read the rules carefully.

There are BRAIN CRUNCHERS on some of the pages. The answers to these are on page 96.

How many letters are there in the word...?

On the road

This game is for two players. It is ideal for playing on a car journey. By adapting the rules and using a dice you could play the game at home (see "Score chart"). You could make the counters shown below before you start playing.

How to play

The aim of this game is to race your opponent to the opposite end of the road.

Start by fixing your counters in the positions shown on the board (keeping them in place with reusable adhesive*). Take turns to spot things from the score chart to move your counter. The number of squares you move are shown on the score chart.

If you land on a white square, your next move must be in the direction shown by the arrow on that square.

How to make counters

Paper

For each counter, trace this picture on paper and glue it to thin cardboard.

Cut around here. — **Cardboard**

Decorate the car, then cut it out as shown.

Bend here. — **Re-usable adhesive**

Bend the counter along the dotted line so that it stands up. Then put some reusable adhesive beneath it.

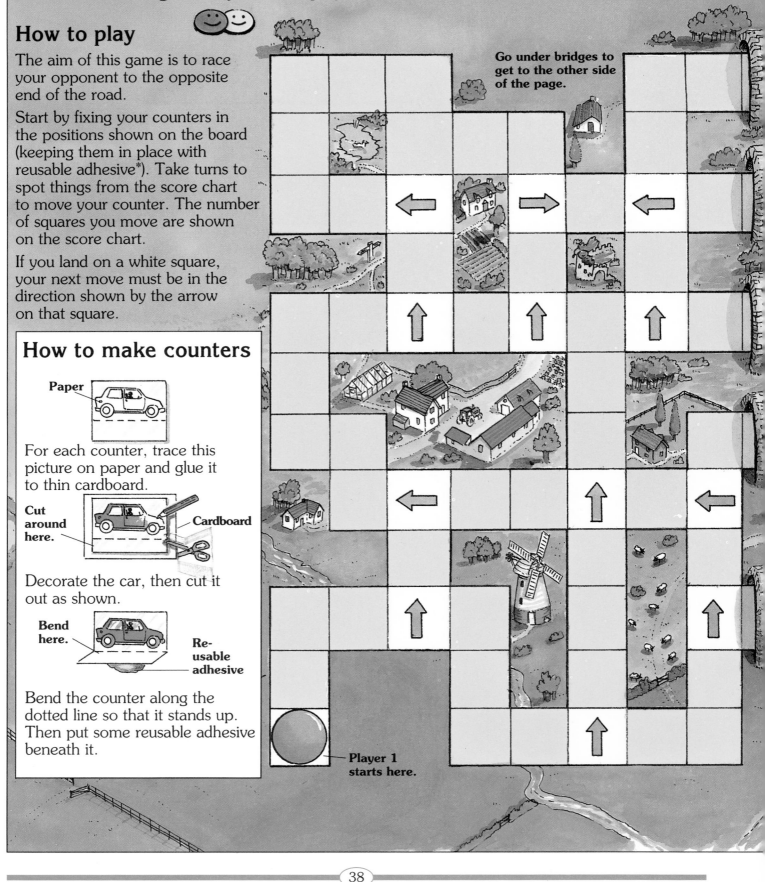

Go under bridges to get to the other side of the page.

Player 1 starts here.

Player 2 starts here.

Score chart

Truck – 1 square

Speed sign – 2 squares

30

Horse – 3 squares

Bridge – 4 squares

Church – 5 squares

Telephone booth – 6 squares

You could make a different score chart to suit your journeys. If you are playing this game at home, take turns throwing a dice, to determine your moves.

Air race

This race is for two players. To play, you will need two counters and a dice. You could make a simple counter by writing your name on a small slip of paper. The winner is the first person to get their plane from Fogsville airport to Cloudsville airport.

How to play

1. Park your counter on one of the departure runways. Take turns throwing the dice. Move your counter the number of squares thrown.

2. You must fly along the route leading from your start square. Follow the flight instructions written on the squares you land on.

3. Some of the squares will divert you onto another route. You can fly along the same route as another plane.

4. If you land on a square that is occupied by your opponent's plane, you must go back to where you were at the start of your move.

5. You must finish on the arrival runway that matches your departure runway, throwing the exact number that you need.

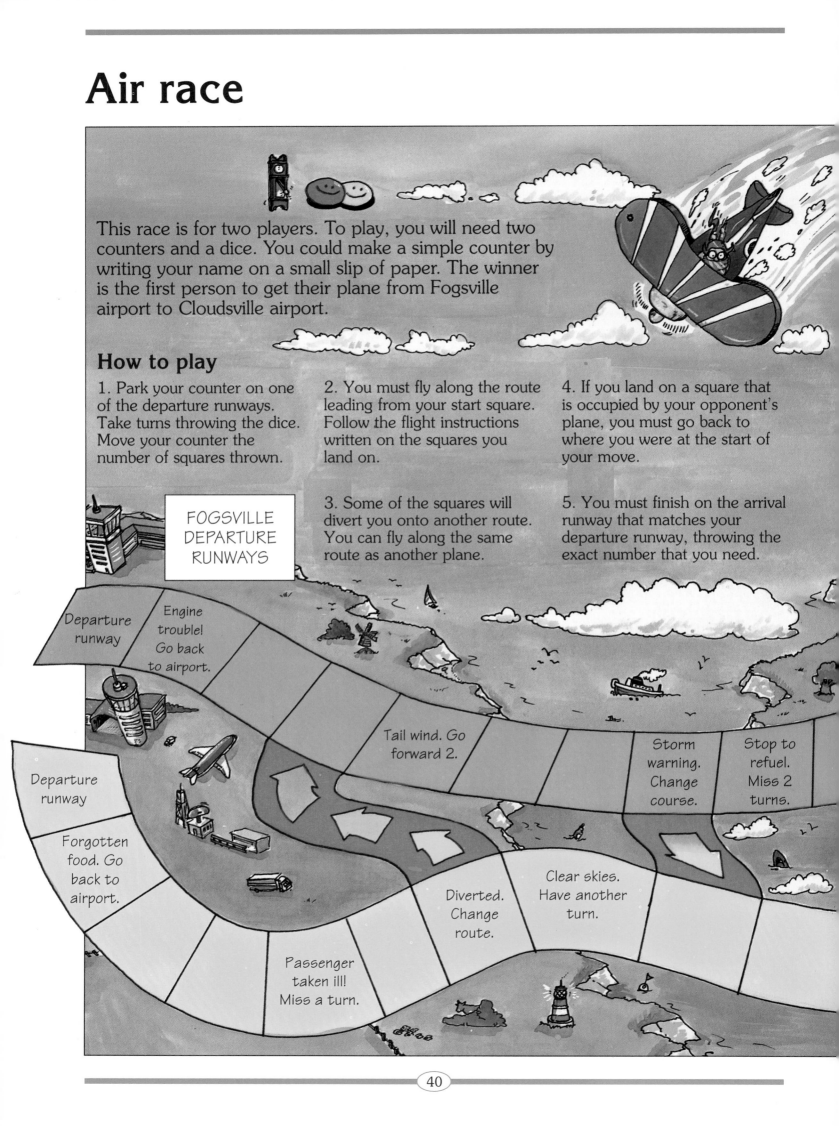

FOGSVILLE DEPARTURE RUNWAYS

Departure runway

Engine trouble! Go back to airport.

Tail wind. Go forward 2.

Storm warning. Change course.

Stop to refuel. Miss 2 turns.

Departure runway

Forgotten food. Go back to airport.

Diverted. Change route.

Clear skies. Have another turn.

Passenger taken ill! Miss a turn.

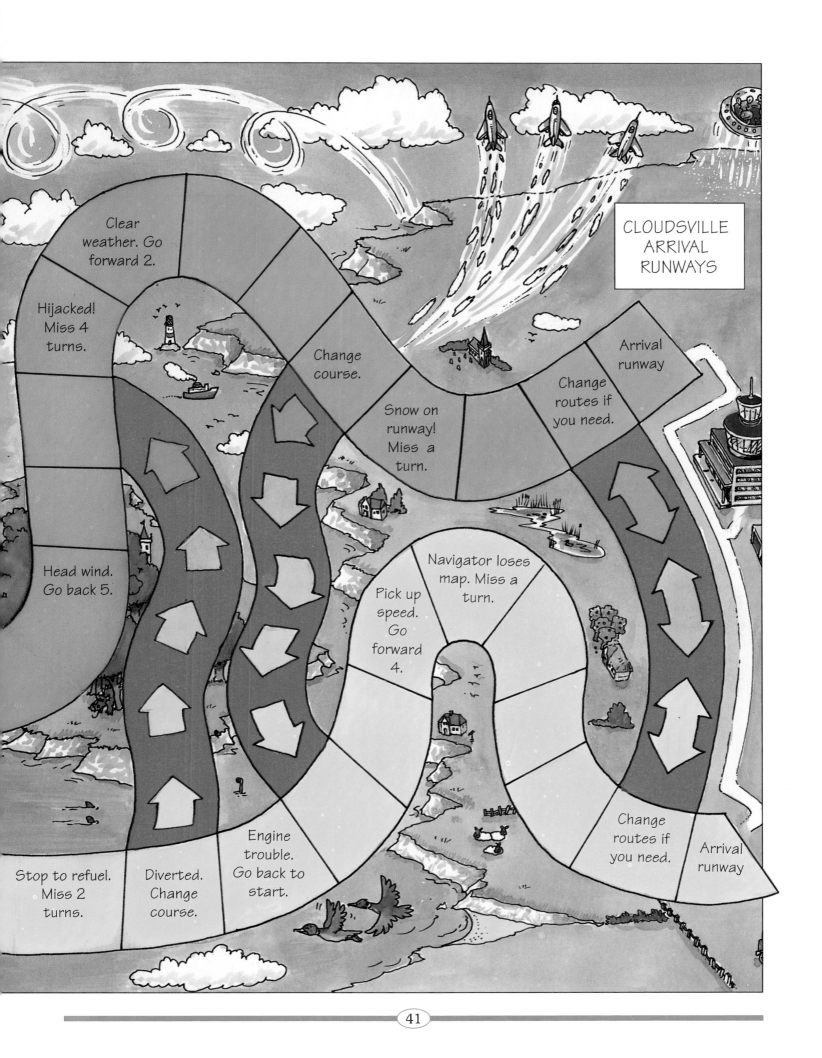

Matchmaker

This is a game for three players. To play, you need three sets of 14 counters, a red set, a green set and a blue set. Before the start, each player chooses which set they want to use.

How to play

To prepare the board, put the blue counters on the dark blue squares, the red counters on the dark red squares and the green counters on the dark green squares.

The aim of the game is to move your counters from their starting squares onto their matching star squares. For example, if you are playing with blue counters, you try to move them to the blue star squares.

Throw the dice to start, then take turns to move. Each turn, move one counter according to the number on the dice. You can move your counters in any direction except diagonally.

You can capture enemy counters by landing on top of them as long as they are not on their own squares (a blue counter on a blue square is safe, for example). When you capture a counter take it off the board. You can't jump over counters.

The game ends when one player has moved all of his or her uncaptured counters to their matching star squares. To calculate the scores, each player counts the number of pieces they have on star squares, adds the number of counters they have captured, and takes away the number of counters that are not on star squares. The player with the highest score is the winner.

BRAIN CRUNCHER

To get from point A to point B on this grid, you can jump from dot to dot in straight lines or diagonally. Can you get from A to B making as many straight jumps as you like, but only three diagonal jumps?

Snakes and ladders

Snakes and ladders is a game for two or more people. You can play using plain counters, but you might like to make counters of your own, featuring pictures of people, animals or other things. There are four characters shown below, which you might like to trace and use.

For long-lasting counters, you could draw the characters onto circles of cardboard.

How to play

Line up the counters at the edge of the board, next to square number 1. Then take turns throwing the dice. When you throw a six put your counter on square number 1. On your next turn, move the number of squares shown on the dice, following the numbers on the board. Every time you throw a six, you can have an extra turn.

If you land at the bottom of a ladder move automatically to the top of the ladder as part of that turn. If you land at the head of a snake move automatically to the bottom of the snake as part of that turn.

Aim to get your piece up to the highest number on the board before your opponents get there. To finish, you must throw the exact number to land on square number 100.

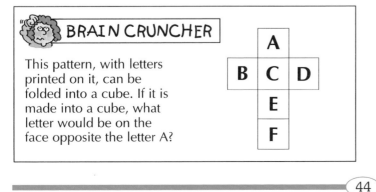

BRAIN CRUNCHER

This pattern, with letters printed on it, can be folded into a cube. If it is made into a cube, what letter would be on the face opposite the letter A?

	A	
B	C	D
	E	
	F	

Aerials and exhausts

This game is for two players. Ideally, you should play it while you are on a car trip, although you can adapt the rules so that you can play it at home, using a dice.

How to play

Hold the book between you. Each choose a start spot and put your finger on it. As soon as you see a car out of the window that has paint which is a similar shade to an aerial leading from the start spot, trace with your finger up the aerial to the next spot. Wait until you see another car.

Go up aerials or down exhausts, from spot to spot, according to the shade of paint on the cars that you see. The first to reach their finishing point is the winner.

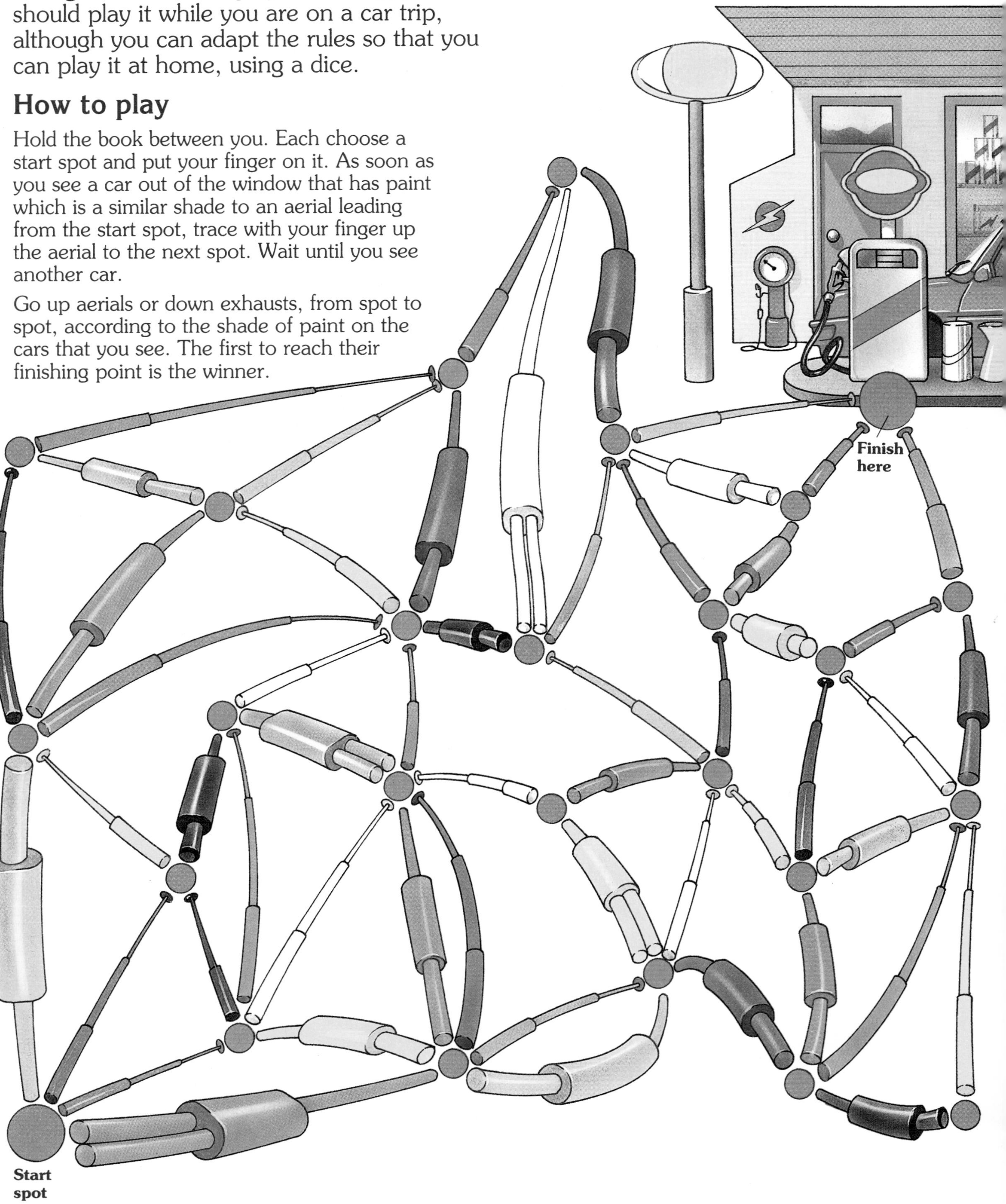

Finish here

Start spot

Extra games ideas

To play at home take turns rolling a dice. Let each number on the dice represent one of the shades featured on the board (such as one for red, two for blue and so on). Count gold and yellow as the same shade so that you have six different shades.

You could challenge your opponent to see who wins the most games in a series of five.

You could play alone and give yourself a time limit to get to the finishing point. Write down the time it takes and see if you can beat your best time.

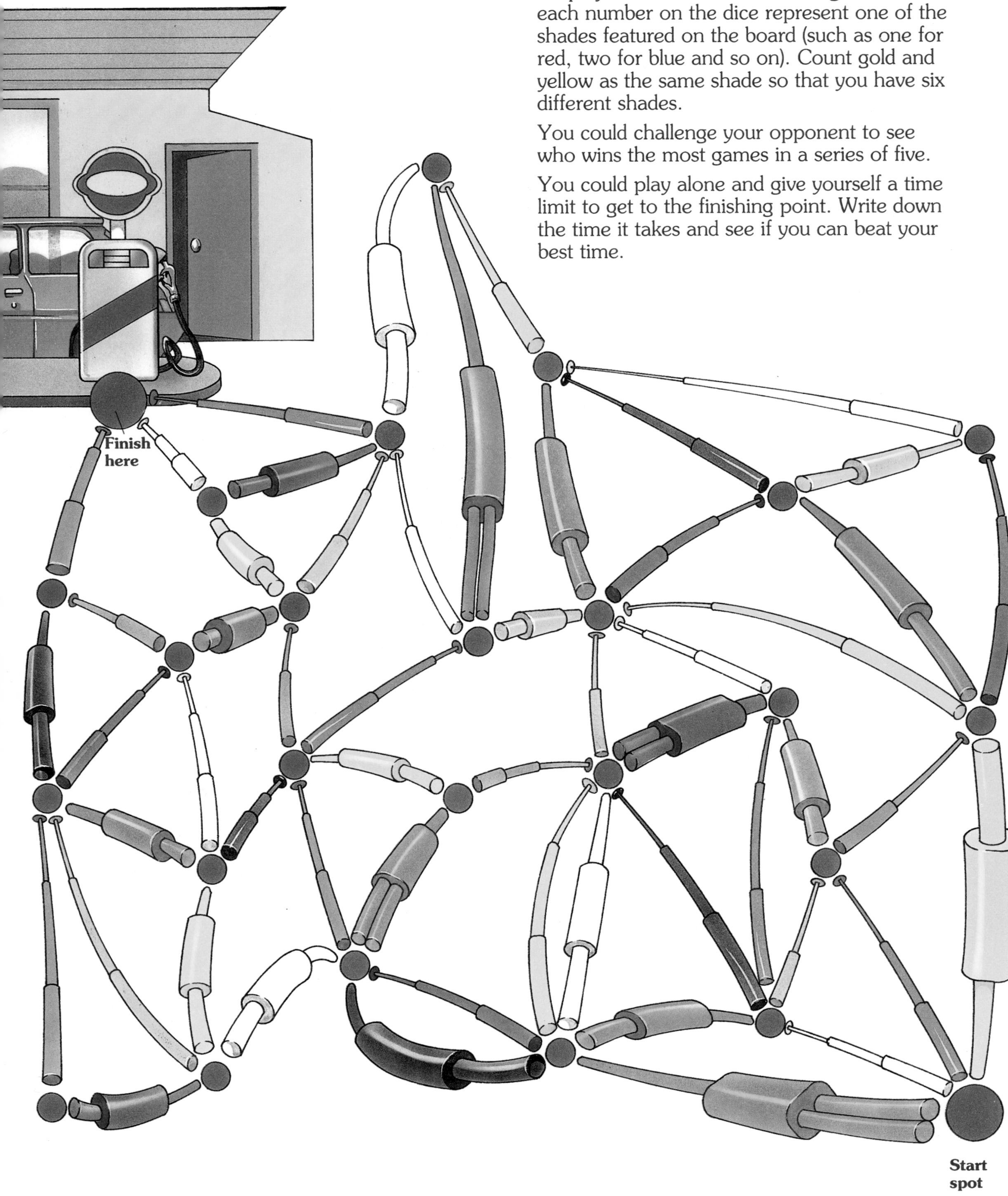

Finish here

Start spot

Spell for your life

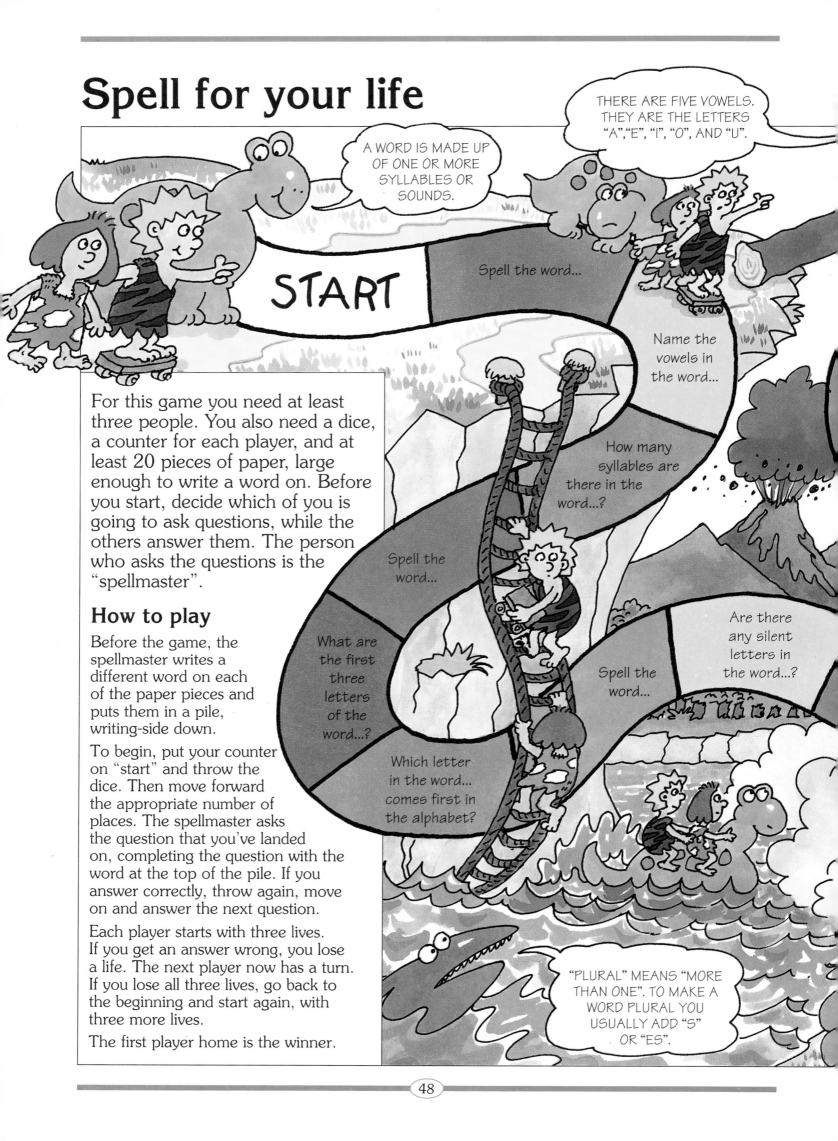

THERE ARE FIVE VOWELS. THEY ARE THE LETTERS "A","E", "I", "O", AND "U".

A WORD IS MADE UP OF ONE OR MORE SYLLABLES OR SOUNDS.

START

Spell the word...

Name the vowels in the word...

How many syllables are there in the word...?

Spell the word...

Are there any silent letters in the word...?

Spell the word...

What are the first three letters of the word...?

Which letter in the word... comes first in the alphabet?

"PLURAL" MEANS "MORE THAN ONE". TO MAKE A WORD PLURAL YOU USUALLY ADD "S" OR "ES".

For this game you need at least three people. You also need a dice, a counter for each player, and at least 20 pieces of paper, large enough to write a word on. Before you start, decide which of you is going to ask questions, while the others answer them. The person who asks the questions is the "spellmaster".

How to play

Before the game, the spellmaster writes a different word on each of the paper pieces and puts them in a pile, writing-side down.

To begin, put your counter on "start" and throw the dice. Then move forward the appropriate number of places. The spellmaster asks the question that you've landed on, completing the question with the word at the top of the pile. If you answer correctly, throw again, move on and answer the next question.

Each player starts with three lives. If you get an answer wrong, you lose a life. The next player now has a turn. If you lose all three lives, go back to the beginning and start again, with three more lives.

The first player home is the winner.

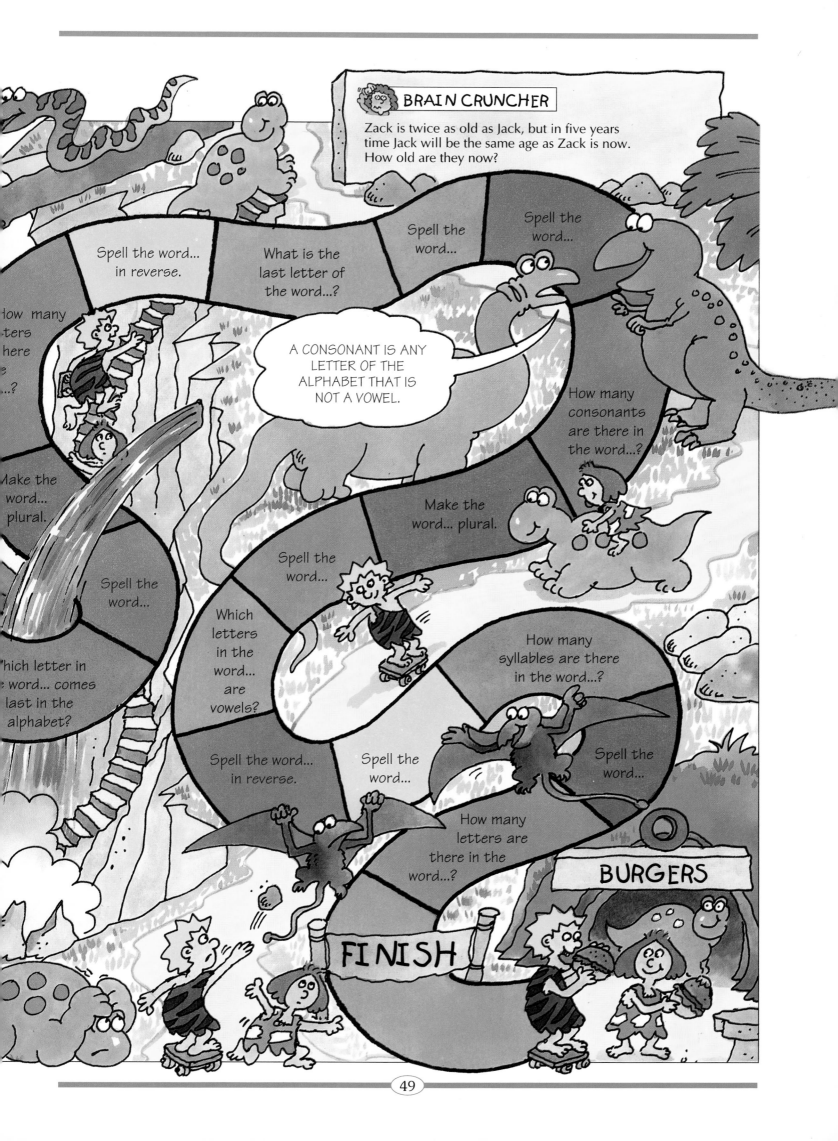

Galaxies

This game is for two or three players. Use counters as spaceships. One player uses three blue counters, one uses three red counters and one uses three green counters. You will need to use three dice.

How to play

The aim is to visit all galaxies from Galaxy 1 to Galaxy 12 in order, before going on to take all three of your spaceships to the finish circles. It's not necessary for all three spaceships to visit all galaxies, but you'll win more points if they do.

When you've moved a ship onto one star in a galaxy, you can take any of your ships to the next one.

To begin, place your ships at the start circle. Take turns throwing the dice. In each turn throw all three dice, but use the score on just one of the dice to move one of your spaceships only. You can choose which ship to move.

Spaceships can move in any direction along the lines. Move one red dot or star for each point.

If you throw the same number on all three dice, have another turn.

No ship can land twice on a dot or star in a turn. No ship can land on the same dot as another ship, or jump over a ship.

How to score

Mark your score after each turn.

If a ship lands on a galaxy star, it scores 1 point. If your second ship lands on a star while the first ship is in the same galaxy, it scores 3 points. If your third ship lands in the same galaxy, it scores 5.

The game ends when a player gets three ships to the finishing circles. Each ship scores 3 points when it finishes.

The scorer of most points wins.

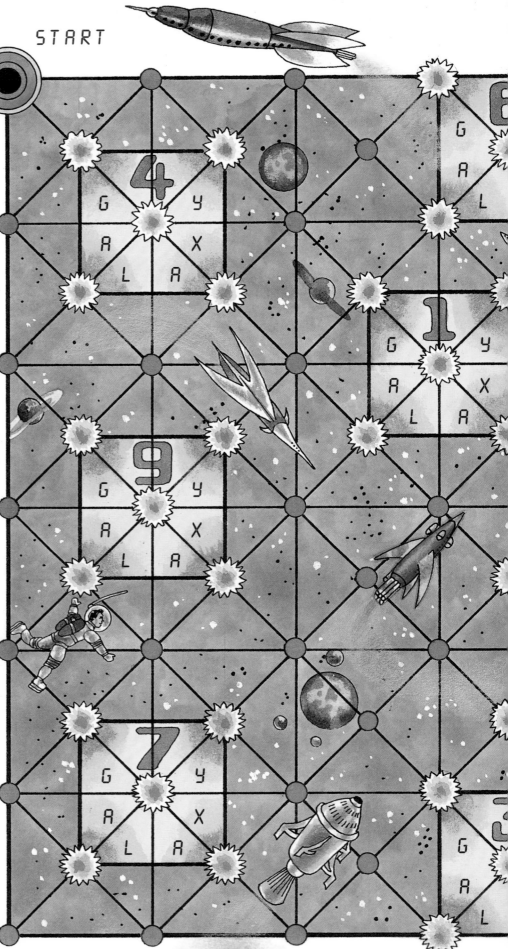

START

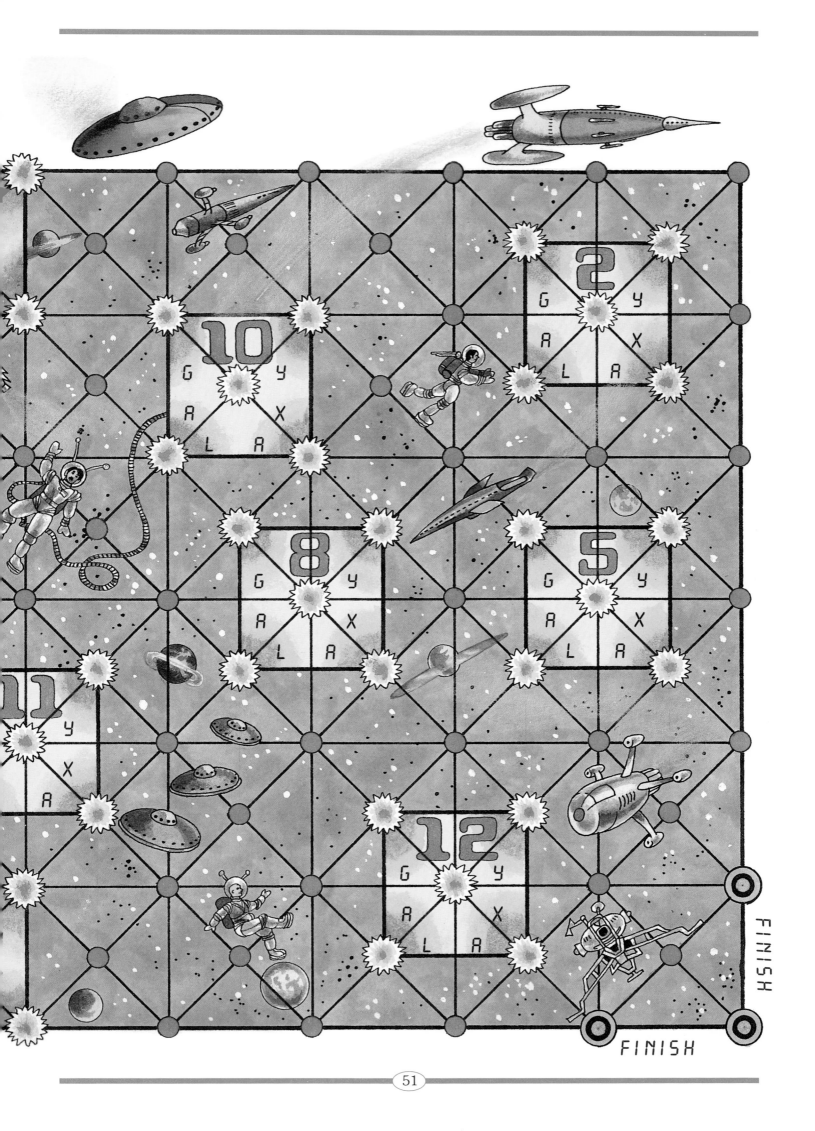

Ludo

Ludo is a game of skill and luck for two, three or four players. Each player has four counters. Either use plain ones or make some of your own, following the designs shown below. You will also need to use a dice. When you play, sit around the book, playing from different sides of the board.

For long-lasting counters, you could draw these designs onto circles of cardboard.

How to play

Before you begin, each player chooses which animal they want to represent – the cat, the snail, the mouse or the frog. The aim of the game is to get all four of your counters around the board and up their ladder to finish at "home" (the little triangle in the middle of the board).

Start with all of your counters in the big square that has a picture of your animal in it. Take it in turns to throw the dice. You must throw a six to bring a counter out onto the board. When you throw a six, put a counter on your starting square (the one with an arrow and a picture of your animal on it.) Then each time it is your turn, you can move your counter around the board in the direction of the arrow, according to the number that you throw on the dice. Each time you throw a six you can have another turn. You must move each counter all the way around the board before you go up the ladder.

You can have as many of your counters out on the board as you like at any time.

If you land on a square occupied by somebody else's counter, their counter has to go right back to the beginning. A player's counter cannot be brought back onto the board until he or she throws a six.

If you land on any picture square that shows your animal, you can move forward three squares. If you land on a square that shows anybody else's animal, move back three squares.

To get a counter home, you must throw the exact number needed to reach the middle triangle.

The winner is the first person to get all of their counters home.

Haunted castle game

This game, for two players, is based on a plan of a haunted castle. Before you start playing you will need to make the board bigger by copying it at a larger size. You might like to enlarge it on a photocopier* and decorate it using bright felt-tip pens. Then copy the treasure counters shown on the right and put one in each of the rooms, except the Dungeon.

Draw the pieces on paper using felt-tips and cut them out.

How to play

In this game each player has a counter that represents a character, such as Black Princess and Red Magician (you can choose other characters if you prefer).

The object of the game is to race one another around the castle, collecting objects from the various rooms that you go into.

Use two different shades of counters to represent the objects, showing their different values. For example, pink is worth 4 points, while yellow is worth 2 points. Place the objects in rooms around the castle before you begin.

Choose which character you want to be, and place your counter at the start door.

Throw a dice to move. You must throw a six to start.

If you land on a yellow door, you can enter the room and pick up the object.

You can move to any room if you land on a red trap door, but in return you must throw the dice to take a "risk".

When all objects have been picked up, race to the Treasure Chest. The game ends when this is collected. The player with the best score wins.

RISK

Go back to the start. Put all your treasure back where it came from.

Spook locks you in the dungeon. Miss a turn.

Ghost gives you the goblet.

Drop one of your objects.

Go to the kitchens for a snack.

Get chained up in the dungeon. Miss two turns.

Put the Treasure Chest in the Turret Room. It is worth six points.

The corridors are made up of equal squares.

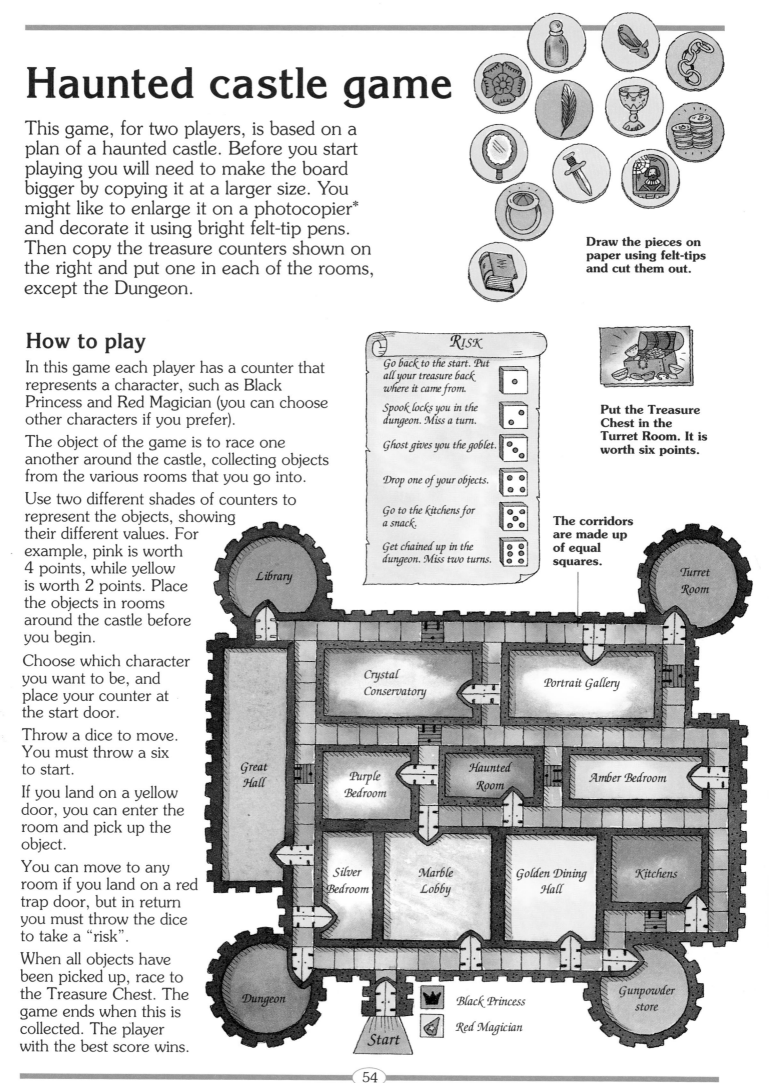

Library

Turret Room

Crystal Conservatory

Portrait Gallery

Great Hall

Purple Bedroom

Haunted Room

Amber Bedroom

Silver Bedroom

Marble Lobby

Golden Dining Hall

Kitchens

Dungeon

Gunpowder store

Start

Black Princess

Red Magician

***You can use photocopiers in public libraries.**

MAZE PUZZLES

Before you try to solve these puzzles, read the short stories that go with them. Then try to find your way through the mazes.

Draw the paths that you choose onto some tracing paper, placed on the pictures.

On some pages there are extra questions, to test your powers of observation. The solutions to these, and the correct routes through the mazes, are on pages 90-92.

BRAIN CRUNCHER questions will also test you throughout the section. The answers to these are on page 96.

NESTING SEASON
Do not disturb the baby animals

Creepy canyon

Cat and Mouse bought cut-price tickets to fly to a distant land for a week. On the plane they were both given parachutes. As they neared their destination, the flight attendant opened the door of the plane and pushed them out. "Have a nice vacation," she smiled. "Now I understand why the tickets were cut-price," groaned Mouse.

They have landed on the edge of a deep canyon. All they can see, in every direction, is desert. After a while, they spot a camel and a camel trader on the other side of the canyon.

Can you help them find the way across the canyon to the camel?

Can you spot four green snakes lurking in the picture?

Can you see a treasure chest?

BRAIN CRUNCHER

In the course of a 24-hour day, how many times does a watch's second hand go past 12?

57

Spacey swamp

Archie the Astronaut and his companions are on Puzzle Planet. They have come across an accident. An alien has crashed her space rocket into a slimy swamp.

Archie is an expert on swamps. He knows that there is only one safe way to cross. They must step from one plant, creeper or creature to another. But they mustn't tread on anything with red spots. They will have to be very careful.

Can you see a way for them to rescue the alien and reach the other side of the swamp?

BRAIN CRUNCHER

"I am going to a party," says Lizzie. "It is my mother's brother's daughter's birthday party." What relation is Lizzie to the person whose party it is?

HANG ON!

Shipwreck

While scuba diving, Cat and Mouse have come across a conger eel, who calls herself Queen Conger. "What are you doing in my kingdom?" she asks. Mouse explains that they are looking for the wreck of an old ship called the Angry Kipper.

Queen Conger tells them where the wreck is. She warns them that they'll have to swim through underwater pathways. Also, they must avoid the tail-biting sharks along the way. They must always swim past the seaweed, not through it, because of the poisonous nose-nippers that live in it.

Can you show Cat and Mouse how to get to the Angry Kipper wreck?

Can you spot a snake wearing a snorkel in the picture?

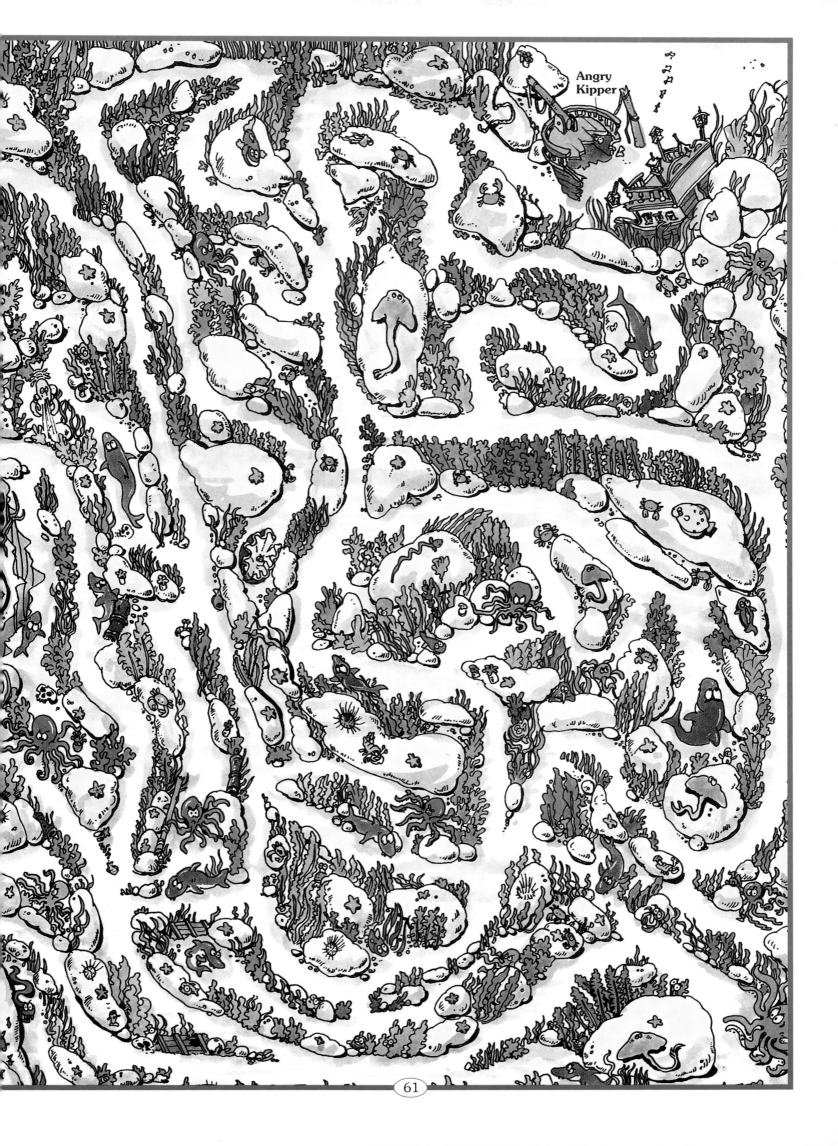

Angry
Kipper

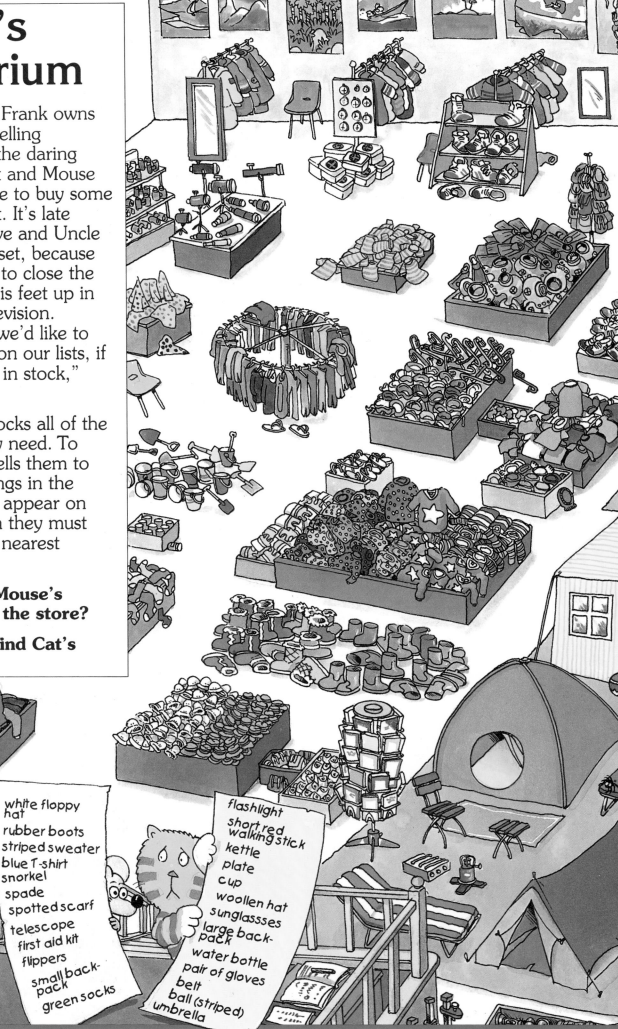

Frank's Emporium

Mouse's Uncle Frank owns an emporium selling everything for the daring adventurer. Cat and Mouse have gone there to buy some new equipment. It's late when they arrive and Uncle Frank looks upset, because he was hoping to close the store and put his feet up in front of the television. "Uncle Frank, we'd like to buy the things on our lists, if you have them in stock," says Mouse.

Uncle Frank stocks all of the things that they need. To save time, he tells them to pick up the things in the order that they appear on their lists. Then they must meet up at the nearest mirror.

Can you find Mouse's route through the store?

Now can you find Cat's route?

white floppy hat
rubber boots
striped sweater
blue T-shirt
snorkel
spade
spotted scarf
telescope
first aid kit
flippers
small back-pack
green socks

flashlight
short red walking stick
kettle
plate
cup
woollen hat
sunglassses
large back-pack
water bottle
pair of gloves
belt
ball (striped)
umbrella

Mouse reaches the mirror first. While he waits for Cat, Uncle Frank calls to him, "I've hung my jacket up somewhere. Can you see it? It has rainbow stripes on it."

Can you help Mouse to find Uncle Frank's missing jacket?

Can you see a spider somewhere in this picture?

63

Leafy lake

Sam the treasure hunter is on a tropical island, searching for gold buried by pirates hundreds of years ago. However, his path is blocked by a big lake. He can't go around the lake because he can't squeeze past the prickly branches of the trees and bushes that grow around its edge.

The lake is covered with lots of giant leaves. Sam knows that he can use them as stepping stones to hop across the lake. But some of the leaves are animals' nests, and some of the leaves have holes in them. He mustn't hop on any of these.

Can you find a way across the lake by hopping from one leaf to another?

NESTING
SEASON
Do not disturb
the baby animals

BRAIN CRUNCHER

Can you cut this cake into eight equal-sized pieces using only three cuts of the knife?

Save Mouse

"Help," cries Mouse. "I'm stuck! HELP!!" While visiting a creepy castle, Mouse has gone into the dungeon. Now he's in trouble. "I warned him not to go down there," moans Cat as he runs down the stairs to help his friend.

As he goes through the door into the dungeon he sees the problem. Mouse is stuck in a monster spider's cobweb, about to be eaten.

Can you show Cat a safe way across the pool of slime to the broken pillar at the bottom of the cobweb? He has a piece of plank which he can use to help him.

BRAIN CRUNCHER

In this plan of a tennis court there are more than eleven rectangles. True or false?

Mouse warns Cat that the red strands of the web are really sticky. He must climb very carefully to avoid waking the giant spider in the corner.

Can you show Cat how to rescue Mouse without stepping on a red strand in the scary spider's cobweb?

Funny mushrooms

Cat and Mouse are staying in a creepy hotel for the weekend. They've been accidentally locked out but have found an open window. Peering in, they can see a room full of funny mushrooms.

Cat knocks a cactus onto a type of mushroom that gives off poisonous dust when it is touched.
Can you help them to find a way across the room to the door that avoids stepping on any dusty mushrooms?

Surf Crab's hut

Cat and Mouse have gone to visit Surf Crab, their old seaside friend. His hut is perched on the end of a rickety pier. Cat and Mouse can see Crab's fishing rod, but he doesn't seem to hear their shouts. They will have to climb along the rotten and unsafe wood of the pier, using the rocks and boats to help them (they can't untie the boats though).

Can you help them to find their way?

Can you spot a snake that's wearing sunglasses, lurking somewhere in this picture?

Puzzling parrots

Cat and Mouse are looking for Pandora Parrot, who lives in this tree with her friends. "I've never met her so I don't know what she looks like," says Cat. Mouse shows Cat a photo of Pandora, to help him.

Using Mouse's picture to help you, can you see Pandora in the tree?

"I can see her!" shouts Mouse. "She's near the top of the tree, looking angry. I'll climb up to see her." The other parrots will not move to let Mouse by. He must climb carefully, crossing from one branch to another where they touch.

Which way should Mouse climb to reach Pandora?

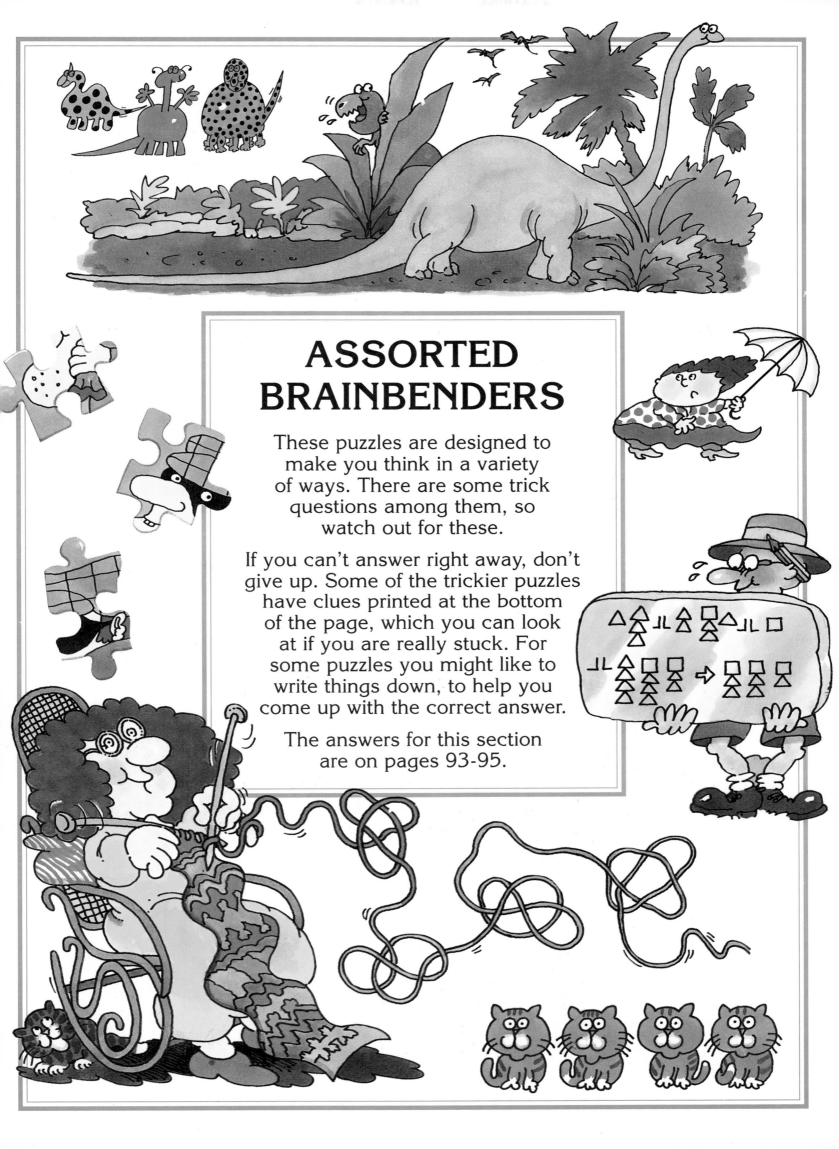

ASSORTED BRAINBENDERS

These puzzles are designed to make you think in a variety of ways. There are some trick questions among them, so watch out for these.

If you can't answer right away, don't give up. Some of the trickier puzzles have clues printed at the bottom of the page, which you can look at if you are really stuck. For some puzzles you might like to write things down, to help you come up with the correct answer.

The answers for this section are on pages 93-95.

Close-up puzzle

Which of these close-up drawings of parts of a face belong to the face shown below?

Count the triangles

Can you find more than 30 triangles in this picture?

Odd shoe

These shoes all look similar, but one is slightly different from the others. **Which is the odd one out?**

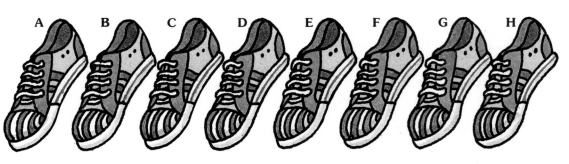

A   B   C   D   E   F   G   H

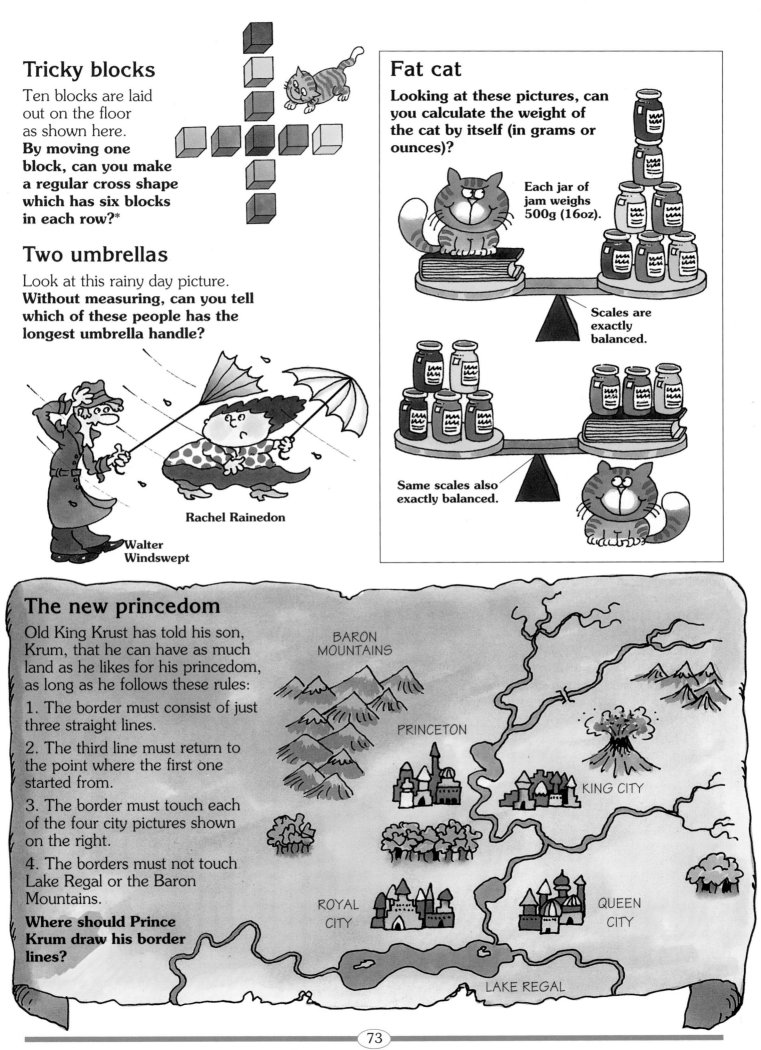

Tricky blocks

Ten blocks are laid out on the floor as shown here. **By moving one block, can you make a regular cross shape which has six blocks in each row?***

Two umbrellas

Look at this rainy day picture. **Without measuring, can you tell which of these people has the longest umbrella handle?**

Rachel Rainedon

Walter Windswept

Fat cat

Looking at these pictures, can you calculate the weight of the cat by itself (in grams or ounces)?

Each jar of jam weighs 500g (16oz).

Scales are exactly balanced.

Same scales also exactly balanced.

The new princedom

Old King Krust has told his son, Krum, that he can have as much land as he likes for his princedom, as long as he follows these rules:

1. The border must consist of just three straight lines.

2. The third line must return to the point where the first one started from.

3. The border must touch each of the four city pictures shown on the right.

4. The borders must not touch Lake Regal or the Baron Mountains.

Where should Prince Krum draw his border lines?

BARON MOUNTAINS

PRINCETON

KING CITY

ROYAL CITY

QUEEN CITY

LAKE REGAL

*Clue: You are allowed to pile one block on top of another.

Divide up the cats

Eccentric Aunt Kitty has gone to Katmandu and left her Siamese cats behind. Catriona, Kate and Tom have been given the job of looking after them while she is away. Before she left, Aunt Kitty said that Catriona was to look after half of them, Tom was to look after one third of them, while Kate was to look after one ninth of them.

Their Uncle Albert (who has several Siamese cats of his own) has discovered that Aunt Kitty has 17 cats. None of the cats can be given away, or shared, so what can they do?

After a few minutes of thought Uncle Albert works out the solution.
What do you think Uncle Albert has decided?*

Marshalling maze

Marshals guide planes to parking bays at Quiztrea International Airport. They use sticks or batons to make direction signals for pilots to follow. Some of the signals are shown on the right.
Following the nine unmarked signals on the right, which parking bay is the plane in the picture below being directed to?
(Imagine you are the pilot looking out of the front of the aircraft.)

Move ahead   Turn right   Turn left   Stop!

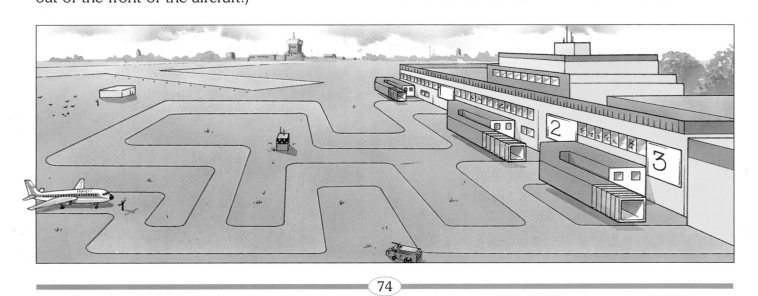

Which face is next?

Below is a series of faces. **Which of the faces in the second row should come next in the series?**

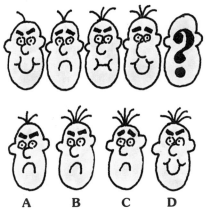

A   B   C   D

Air acrobatics

This team of airborne acrobats are doing a daring trick. **Can you see how they made the second pyramid from the first by moving only three acrobats?**

Pyramid problem

Can you calculate how many blocks were needed to build this pyramid (including the one that is about to be hoisted into position)? The blocks are all the same size.

Crossed lines

Four inexperienced fishermen have gone fishing. **What has each of them caught?**

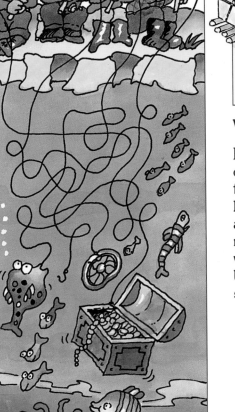

Weigh the boxes

Here are six boxes, all exactly the same size. One of the matching pairs of boxes weighs more than the other two pairs.

How can you find out which are the heavier boxes by making only one weighing on the balancing scales shown below?

Orange puzzler

There are six oranges in this bag.
How can you give these people an orange each and still have one left in the bag?

Cross-number puzzle

Can you fill in this number puzzle, by working out the multiplying problems shown below it?

Across

1. 6 x 6	8. 5 x 9
3. 5 x 4	9. 7 x 10
4. 6 x 5	10. 9 x 6
6. 3 x 11	12. 10 x 2
7. 9 x 5	13. 2 x 11

Down

2. 7 x 9	8. 11 x 4
3. 9 x 3	9. 8 x 9
5. 7 x 11	10. 10 x 5
6. 7 x 5	11. 2 x 6
7. 4 x 10	

On the roof

Below is a map of the roof of a building. On the right are four views taken from the spot marked X on the map, facing north, south, east and west.
Judging from the pictures and the map, can you decide which view is which?

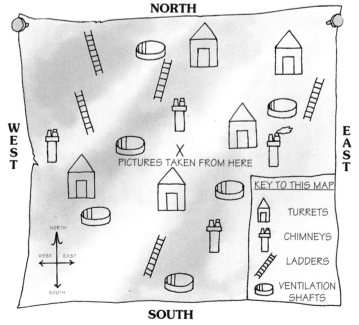

Where in the chairs?

Although you can't see them from behind, there are people sitting in some of these chairs.
Can you calculate the smallest number of occupied chairs from the information on the right?

A boy is sitting on the right of a girl.

A girl is sitting on the right of a girl.

Two girls are sitting on the left of a boy.

What shade?

If all odd numbers are red and all even numbers are blue, what shade is an odd number plus an even number?

Party puzzler

Which of the tables on the right is laid exactly like the one at the party described by the four people below?

Jim said there was a big cake with pink icing and six chocolate drops on top. There was a plate of square sandwiches too. The table was covered with a red striped cloth.

Fred said there were triangular sandwiches. Next to these, on the right, there was a large red jelly.

Judy said the jelly was green and there were square chocolate cookies.

Sue said she loved the cupcakes with cherries on top. There were six of them. She thought that the tablecloth had yellow spots on it.

Eric said the large cake was covered with white icing. There were no chocolate cookies and the sandwiches were horrible.

Later, Eric said that he had not told the truth and Judy said she had confused the party with another one. The other three were right.

Clare's cousins

This is a picture of Clare with some of her family and friends.

Clare's grandmother on her father's side had two children, who each had two children. Her grandmother on her mother's side also had two children. They, too, each had two children.

Can you work out how many cousins Clare has?

Parking spaces

A stadium has parking spaces for 5000 cars. There are 4250 cars parked in it at the moment, 30 minutes before the big game starts.

Which of the signs below shows how many spaces are left?

If 25 cars can park every minute, how many cars will be parked when the game starts?

251 SPACES

559 SPACES

750 SPACES

How many cubes?

Which of these shapes, if folded along the dotted lines, could be made into cubes?

This is what a cube looks like.

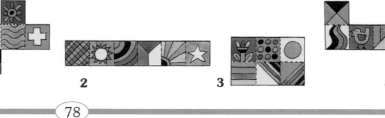

1   2   3   4

Nine question

How many times can you subtract the first number from the second one?

Dinoburgers

Judging from this picture, even prehistoric people liked burgers. This caveperson is buying a brontoburger. So far the seller has sold 1224 brontoburgers, 785 tyrannoburgers and 643 vegetarian swampburgers.

How many burgers has he sold altogether?

How many more meat burgers than vegetarian burgers has he sold?

Doodlesaurs

Below are three Doodlesaurs, incredible monsters from Planet Strange.

Below are three more incredible creatures. However, they are not Doodlesaurs.

Which of these monsters are Doodlesaurs?

Who did it?

Someone has broken Mrs. Grump's window. Of her three suspects, only one is telling the truth; the other two are lying.

Who broke the window?*

I DIDN'T

BOB DID

ROCKY IS LYING.

Cassie

Rocky

Bob

Clue: Try each person's response in turn and check to see if they can be telling the truth.

Mend the broken necklace

Can you mend this necklace by working out in which order the spare beads should be threaded?

Add beads to this end.

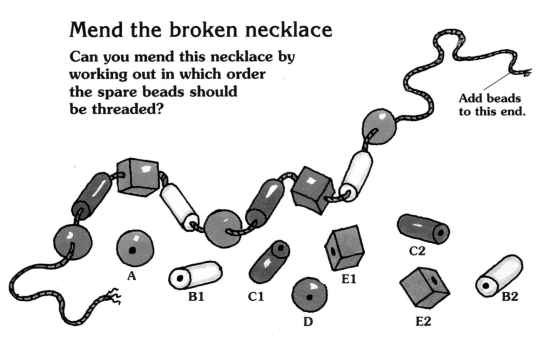

A   B1   C1   D   E1   E2   C2   B2

Hole puzzle

If two people dig four holes in eight days, how long does it take one person to dig a hole?

Jigsaw pieces

In this jigsaw puzzle, can you decide which piece goes next to which to make a complete picture?

A   B   C   D   E   F

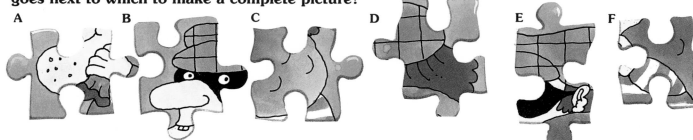

The odd number

Which of these numbers is the odd one out?

18   75   39   47   51

Quick question

What is half of two divided by a half?

Value for money

Which of these packets of alien chocolates should this hungry alien buy, so that he gets the best value for his Martian money? In Martian money there are 50 moons in 1 dragon.

?

NOW ONLY 50 MOONS A PACKET

MARSCHOCS 40 CHOCS

SPECIAL OFFER 2 PACKS FOR 1 DRAGON 40 MOONS

30 CHOCS   30 CHOCS

Find the key

Only one of the keys on the left will fit the lock design shown below. **Which one?**

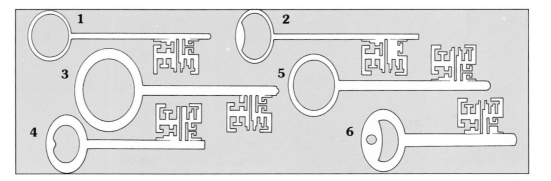

Which house fits the plan?

Below is a plan of the ground floor of a house. **Can you work out which of these houses it belongs to?**

How big is the dinosaur?

This dinosaur's tail is twice as long as its body, which is half as long as its neck (to the end of its nose), which is 12m (40ft) long. **What does the dinosaur measure from nose to tail?**

Will Mouse get the cheese?

What will happen to Mouse if he stays where he is and Cat continues to turn the large wheel in the direction you can see here?

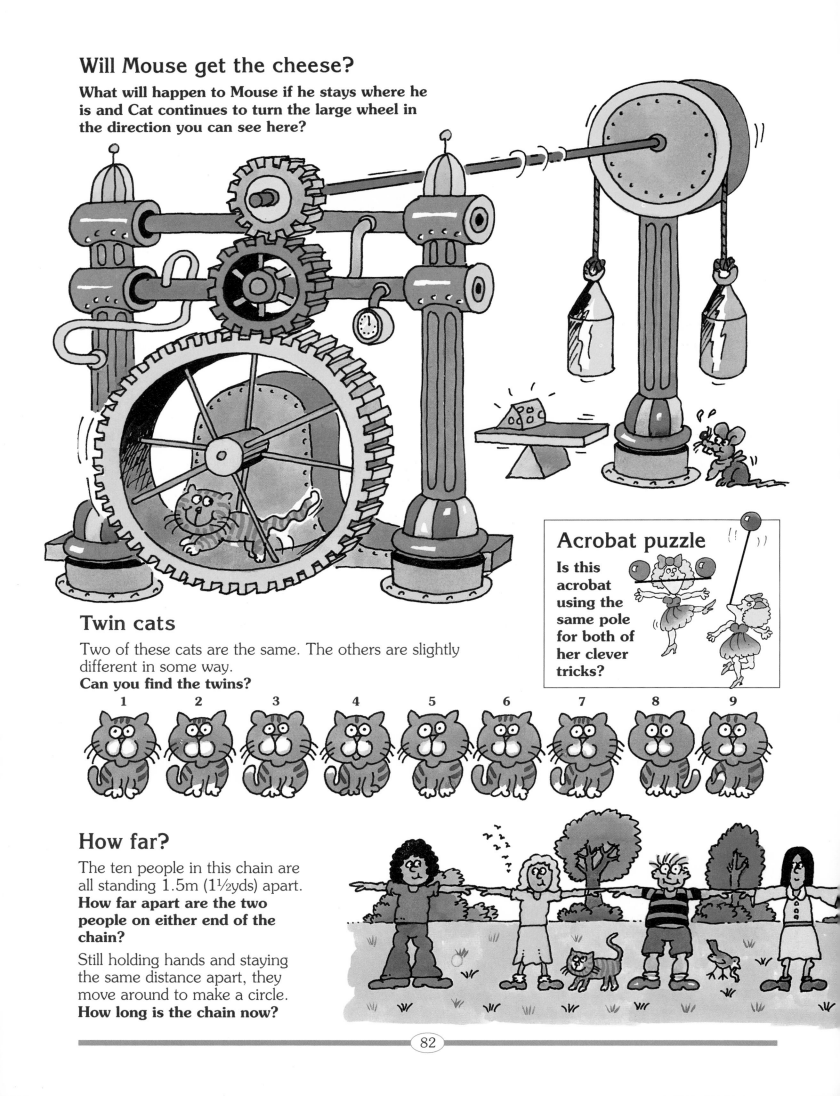

Acrobat puzzle

Is this acrobat using the same pole for both of her clever tricks?

Twin cats

Two of these cats are the same. The others are slightly different in some way.
Can you find the twins?

1 2 3 4 5 6 7 8 9

How far?

The ten people in this chain are all standing 1.5m (1½yds) apart.
How far apart are the two people on either end of the chain?

Still holding hands and staying the same distance apart, they move around to make a circle.
How long is the chain now?

Number jigsaw

Can you fit the four spare pieces into the spaces in the puzzle?
When it is complete, the numbers must add up to 15 in every direction.

Which letter?

Which of the spare cards should the middle person be holding?

Eggs puzzle

Each of these three friends wants an egg every day. The three hens they have lay three eggs in three days.
How many more hens do they need?

Missing shapes

The shapes shown here form a series.
Can you tell which of the shapes marked 1-4 is missing from the middle of the series?

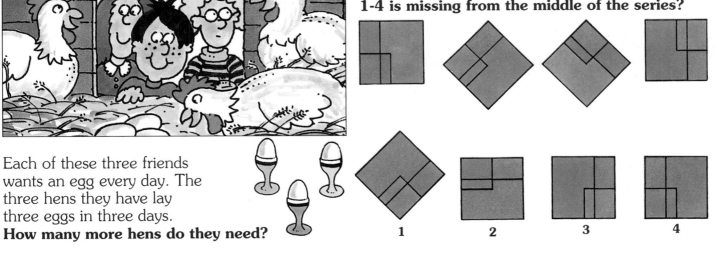

Escaped zoo animals

Seven zebras, four monkeys, three camels, an elephant and five giraffes escaped from the zoo. On each of the following days, half of the animals on the loose were recaptured.

How many animals were free at the end of the second day?

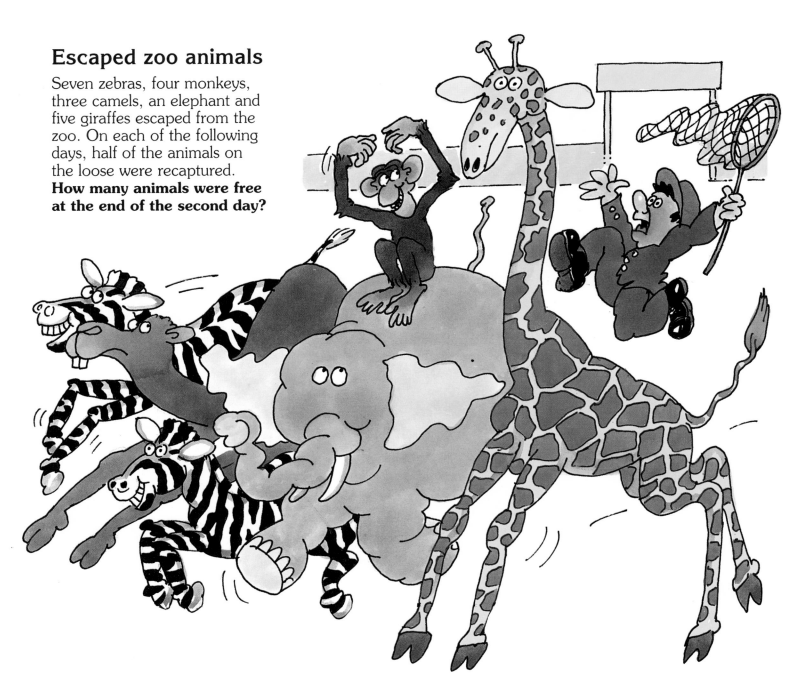

Soccer shirts

Puzzletown Hotshots soccer club has enough players for two teams of eleven players, with six reserves for each team. Their shirts are numbered, on the front only, from 1 to 34.

How many figure ones are needed for their new set of shirts?

Which cat?

Which of the cats numbered 1 to 4 below should come next in the row on the wall?

1   2   3   4

Knotty knitter

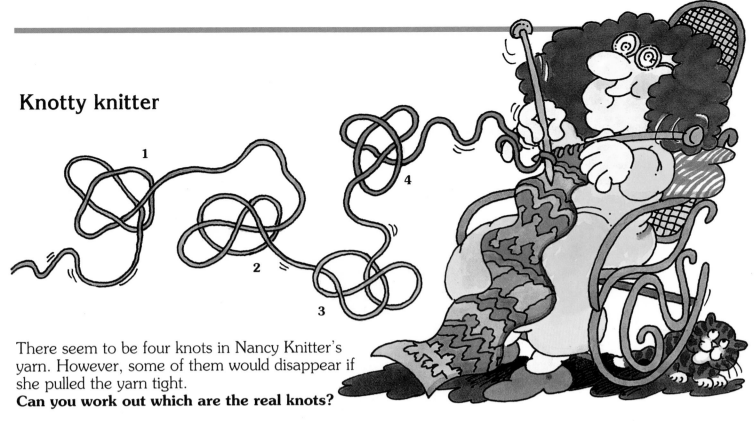

There seem to be four knots in Nancy Knitter's yarn. However, some of them would disappear if she pulled the yarn tight.
Can you work out which are the real knots?

Ancient arithmetic

Archie Ologist, the scientist, has dug up an old clay tablet used by the ancient King Tutt-tutt when he was at school, thousands of years ago. Archie has worked out that:

means =

means 1

means 5

means 7

Can you translate what is on the tablet?

Fit the food

From these clues, can you decide which food tray belongs to which customer?

Tiny Tim wants ice cream, but no hot drink.

Bearded Bill wants French fries, but no sausages.

Slick-haired Simon wants sausages, but no ice cream.

Betty Birdhat wants a hot drink, but no French fries.

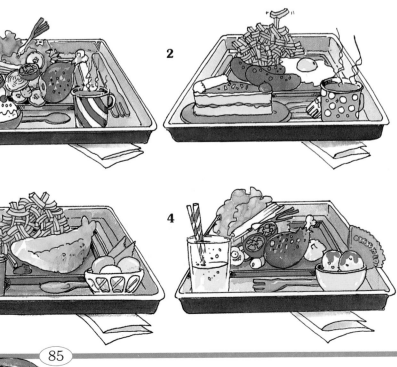

Which button?

Spaceman Sam has been trapped in a room with a time bomb by some naughty aliens. He has 7.38 minutes to find out which button opens the door.

He knows that the buttons are numbered from 1 to 16, with no number appearing twice. He also knows that the numbers in each row, column and diagonal add up to 34.

To open the door, he must press button number 1. All other buttons will trigger the bomb.
Where on the panel is button number 1?

Which cog?

Suzie Sprocket needs a new cog wheel for her bike. She knows that it must have ten square teeth and a round hole in the middle. The man in the shop has told her to sort through this box. **Which one should she buy?**

Next number

Here are some members of Franky Fit's soccer team. The numbers on their shirts form a series. **Can you tell which number the end player should wear on his shirt?**

Another next number

Can you tell what number the player on the right of this row should have on his shirt?

Two train teaser

A local train, consisting of an engine and an old carriage, is holding up the Express by stopping at every station.

At last, it reaches a station with a siding. The siding is small, however. It can hold only one carriage or an engine, not both at once.

Can you decide what the trains should do in order to pass each other?*

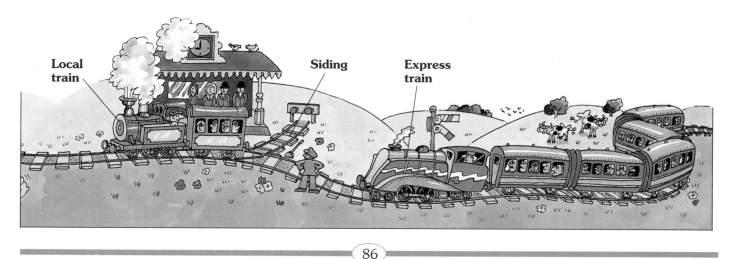

Local train

Siding

Express train

*Clue: You will need to move both trains back and forward along the track several times.

Who is right?

These Martians are out spotting wildlife and making notes about what they see. The pages from their notebooks are shown on the right, below. Only one of them has identified all the creatures in this picture correctly.

Using this page from the *Nature Guide to Mars*, can you tell who is correct?

Three cats

Which of these cats is the biggest?
Guess first, then measure to see if you were right

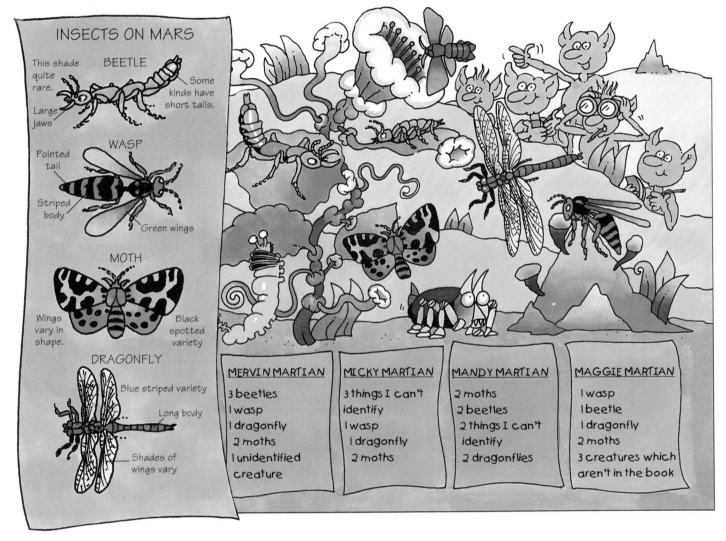

INSECTS ON MARS

BEETLE
This shade quite rare.
Large jaws
Some kinds have short tails.

WASP
Pointed tail
Striped body
Green wings

MOTH
Wings vary in shape.
Black spotted variety

DRAGONFLY
Blue striped variety
Long body
Shades of wings vary

MERVIN MARTIAN
3 beetles
1 wasp
1 dragonfly
2 moths
1 unidentified creature

MICKY MARTIAN
3 things I can't identify
1 wasp
1 dragonfly
2 moths

MANDY MARTIAN
2 moths
2 beetles
2 things I can't identify
2 dragonflies

MAGGIE MARTIAN
1 wasp
1 beetle
1 dragonfly
2 moths
3 creatures which aren't in the book

Dead end puzzle

Four workmen have trapped themselves in an alley. Unfortunately, the ones in blue hats are too large to get out through the space behind them.

The men in red hats could get out if they could get past the men in blue hats. There is a doorway between them, which is big enough for one person to stand in at a time.

Can you see how the two workmen in red hats can get out of the alley before the blockage is removed?
The diagram on the right of the page should help you to see the solution.

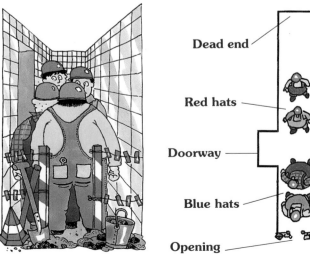

Dead end

Red hats

Doorway

Blue hats

Opening

Answers to Picture puzzles

Pages 22-23

Archie and his assistant have landed in a wild and scary part of Puzzle Planet, as shown by the blue volcano, orange pool and the trees that are outlined in red.

Page 24

13 of Wizard Wilf's friends drank his magic grog. They are all circled in blue.

Page 25

The ten things that have disappeared from Wizard Wilf's den are circled in green.

Pages 26-27

The shops that Katy and Tim must go to are circled in red.

The flower shop is unusual because its front door is high above the ground.

The balloon thief is circled in blue.

Pages 28-29

Gretel's lost goats are circled in red.

The lost ice skate is circled in blue.

Not including the goats, there are four horned creatures in the picture. They are circled in green.

Pages 30-31

The seven blue bananas are circled in red.

Pages 32-33

Mechanic Molly's lost tools are all circled in red.

The twelve animals are circled in green.

Pages 34-35

The types of chair that the people should sit in are indicated on the right.

There are 19 hats in the picture. They are circled in red.

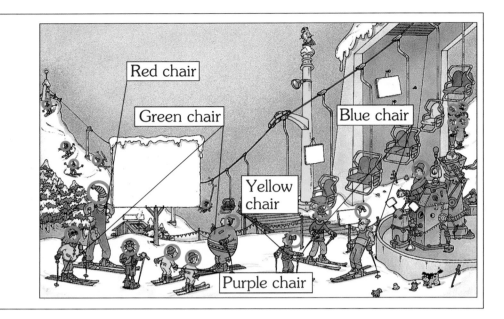

Page 36

Ghost	pages 24 and 25	Eggs in a nest	page 29
Half-eaten cookie	page 32	Snowman destroyer	page 29
Goofy cat	pages 27 and 32	Blue creature	pages 28 and 35
Motorcycle and sidecar	page 27	Fish sign	page 27
Bread tree	page 22	Space car	page 22
Crazy snake	page 30	Giant pink marshmallow	page 30
Yellow mushroom	page 22	Mystery box	pages 24 and 25
Ski pole	page 35	Bird of prey	page 35
Yellow fruit	page 31	Red-edged cloak	page 33
Juggling ball	pages 24 and 25		

Answers to Maze puzzles

Pages 56-57

Cat and Mouse's route across the canyon is shown in red.

The four green snakes are circled in blue.

The treasure chest is circled in green.

Pages 58-59

The route that Archie and his friends should take is shown in red.

Pages 60-61

Cat and Mouse should swim through the pathways shown in red to reach the Angry Kipper.

The snake wearing a snorkel is circled in green.

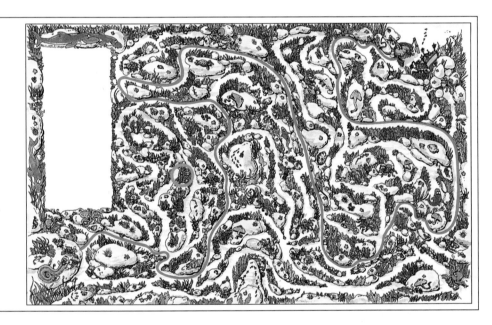

Pages 62-63

Mouse's route through the store is shown in red.

Cat's route is shown in blue.

Uncle Frank's missing jacket is circled in green.

The spider that is lurking in the picture is circled in yellow.

Pages 64-65

Sam's route across the lake is shown in red.

Pages 66-67

The safe way for Cat to get across to the broken pillar is shown in red.

Cat can rescue Mouse by climbing the cobweb according to the route shown in blue.

Page 68

The safe route is shown in red.

Page 69

The route is in red.
The snake is circled in blue.

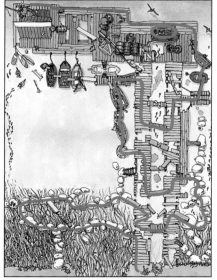

Page 70

Pandora is circled in blue. Mouse should follow the trail shown in red to reach Pandora.

Answers to Assorted brainbenders

Pages 72-73

Close-up puzzle

Pieces 2, 3, 4, 6, 9, 10 and 14 fit the face. The others don't.

Count the triangles

There are at least 31 triangles in the picture. You can see where they are on the picture below. You may be able to find some more but remember that they must be complete triangles.

Odd shoe

Shoe F is the odd shoe.

Tricky blocks

Take a block from the top of the cross and place it on top of the block in the middle. You will have two rows with six blocks in each.

Two umbrellas

The two umbrella handles are the same length.

Fat cat

The cat weighs 2500g (80oz/5lbs).

The new princedom

Here are Prince Krum's borders.

Pages 74-75

Divide up the cats

Uncle Albert will lend one of his cats to the children, so that they have 18 in all. Catriona will be able to look after nine of them, Tom will have six of them and Kate can have two of them. This leaves one spare cat, so they can give it back to Uncle Albert.

Marshalling maze

The plane is being directed to parking bay 3.

Which face is next?

Face B should come next in the row.

Air acrobatics

This is how the acrobats made the second pyramid (shown in green) from the first pyramid (shown in blue).

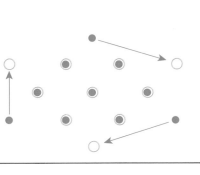

Pyramid problem

30 blocks were needed for the pyramid:
There are 4 x 4 = 16 in the bottom layer.
3 x 3 = 9 in the second layer.
2 x 2 = 4 in the third layer.
and 1 on the top.

Crossed lines

Fisherman 1 caught nothing.
Fisherman 2 caught the box of treasure.
Fisherman 3 caught the wheel.
Fisherman 4 caught the fish.

Weigh the boxes

Weigh a box of one shade, say a red one, against one of another shade, say a blue one. If they balance, then the boxes of the third shade must be the heavier ones. If they don't balance you will be able to see which shade is the heavier from the direction the scale tips.

Page 76-77

Orange puzzler

Take five oranges out of the bag and give one to each of the people. Then give the sixth person the bag containing the orange that is left.

Cross-number puzzle

The puzzle solution looks like this:

On the roof

Picture 1 is the view that you would see if you were facing directly west. Picture 2 is the view facing directly north. Picture 3 is the view facing directly south. Picture 4 is the view facing directly east.

Where in the chairs?

The smallest number of occupied chairs is three. They are shown on the right. (In the descriptions, "left" and "right" are used as if you were looking from the back, as you were in the puzzle.)

What shade?

An odd number plus an even number will produce a number that is red. For example 2 (blue) plus 5 (red) will give 7 (red).

Party puzzler

Table 4 shows what there was to eat at the party.

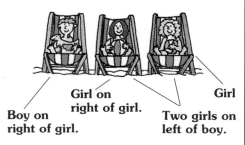

Boy on right of girl.

Girl on right of girl.

Girl

Two girls on left of boy.

Page 78-79

Clare's cousins

Clare has four cousins. Here is her family tree to show you how:

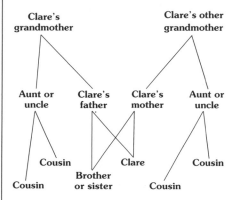

Clare's grandmother

Clare's other grandmother

Aunt or uncle

Clare's father

Clare's mother

Aunt or uncle

Cousin

Clare

Cousin

Cousin

Brother or sister

Cousin

Parking spaces

The sign that shows 750 spaces is correct. 5000 cars will be parked when the game starts.

How many cubes?

Shapes 1 and 4 can be folded up to make cubes.

Nine question

This is a trick question. You can take 9 from 39 only once, because after you have taken 9 away you don't have 39 any more.

Dinoburgers

The burger seller has sold 2652 burgers altogether. He has sold 1366 more meat burgers than vegetarian burgers.

Doodlesaurs

Monsters 2 and 4 are Doodlesaurs.

Who did it?

Cassie did it.

Page 80-81

Mend the broken necklace

The spare beads should be threaded in this order:

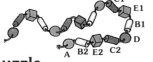

Hole puzzle

It takes one person half a day to dig a hole.

Jigsaw pieces

Here is the completed jigsaw.

The odd number

47 is the odd number. The others can be divided by 3.

Quick question

Half of two divided by a half equals two.

Value for money

The packet that costs 50 moons is the better buy. The special offer gives 60 chocolates for 90 moons. At this rate 40 chocolates costs 60 moons. The separate packet gives 40 chocolates for 50 moons, so it is cheaper.

Find the key

Key number 5 is the only one that fits the lock design.

Which house fits the plan?

House E is the only one that fits the plan.

How big is the dinosaur?

The dinosaur measures 30m (100ft) from nose to tail.

Neck is 12m (40ft)

Body is half neck = 6m (20ft)

Tail is twice body = 12m (40ft)

Page 82-83

Will Mouse get the cheese?

If Cat continues running in the same direction then Mouse will get the cheese, as this picture shows.

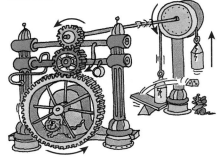

Twin cats

Cats 2 and 6 are the twins.

Acrobat puzzle

The acrobat is using the same pole for both tricks.

How far?

The two people on either end of the chain are 13.5m (13½ yds) apart.

When the people form a circle the chain is 15m (15yds) long.

Number jigsaw

Here is the completed jigsaw.

Which letter?

Letter K. There are three letters between each letter in the series.

Eggs puzzle

The friends need six more hens.

Missing shapes

Shape number 2 is the missing shape.

Page 84-85

Escaped zoo animals

Five animals were still free at the end of the second day.

Soccer shirts

14 figure ones are needed for Puzzletown Hotshots' new set of shirts.

Which cat?

Cat number 4 should come next on the wall.

Knotty knitter

Knots 1 and 3 are real.

Ancient arithmetic

The tablet reads:
13 + 271 + 5 + 487 = 776

Fit the food

Tiny Tim should have tray number 4.
Bearded Bill should have tray number 3.
Slick-haired Simon should have tray number 2.
Betty Birdhat should have tray number 1.

Page 86-87

Which button?

Button number 1 is at the bottom right. The complete panel looks like this:

Which cog?

Suzie Sprocket should buy the red cog in the second row from the top.

Next number

The person at the end should wear number 35. The sequence is:
3 (+5) 8 (+7) 15 (+9) 24 (+11) 35.

Another next number

The person at the end should wear number 5.
The sequence is:
3 (-1) 2 (+2) 4 (-1) 3 (+2) 5.

Two train teaser

This sequence describes what the trains should do in order to pass each other:

1. Local train backs into siding and unhooks carriage.

2. Local train engine moves up the track, clear of the station.

3. Express train moves up past siding, reverses so that end carriage can hook onto spare carriage.

4. Express moves forward pulling spare carriage out of siding with it and then backs off down track again.

5. Local train engine backs into siding.

6. Express train unhooks local carriage, leaves it on track and moves up line beyond station.

7. Local engine comes out of siding and backs down track to pick up its carriage.

Who is right?

Maggie Martian has identified all the creatures correctly.

Three cats

The three cats are all the same size.

Dead end puzzle

This sequence describes how the people in red hats manage to get out:

1. Red hat goes in doorway.

2. Blue hats move down alley past doorway. Red hat in doorway can now get out.

3. Blue hats move back up the alley. Second red hat goes in doorway.

4. Blue hats move back down alley. Red hat can now escape.

BRAIN CRUNCHERS answers

Page 7
Friday.

Page 16 (top)
To keep the goats apart, you'd build the pens like this:

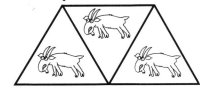

Page 16 (bottom)
The next number in the series is 36.

The secret is to notice that the first number is equal to 2 x 2, the second number is equal to 3 x 3, the third number is equal to 4 x 4, and so on.

Page 22
You had 24 cookies to start with.

Page 25
This is how you'd wrap the string around the pegs to make six squares.

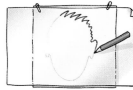

Page 27
In all, you will have 127 grapes.

Page 28
This is where you'd build four new walls to make separate rooms for the office workers:

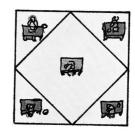

Page 30
There are eight spaces.

Page 33
The car will have gone 4.5km (3 miles) in total.

Page 34
The tunnel route is faster. It takes 25 minutes. The mountain road route takes 30 minutes.

Page 42
This is how you can get from A to B by making only three diagonal jumps.

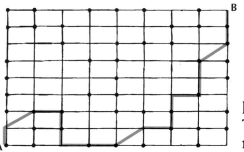

Page 44
The letter E will be on the face that is opposite the letter A.

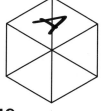

Page 49
Zack is ten. Jack is five.

Page 57
In the course of a 24-hour day the second hand goes past 12 1440 times.

Page 58
Lizzie is the cousin of the person who is having a birthday party.

Page 63
There are 16 squares in the pattern.

Page 65
Here is how you cut the cake three times to make eight equal-sized pieces.

Page 66
True. There are 13 rectangles in all.

Tracing
Tracing is a useful way to copy a picture accurately. This short guide shows you how to make successful tracings.

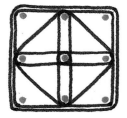

1. Lay tracing paper over the picture that you want to trace. Attach the paper to the picture. Trace the outline with a pencil.

2. Remove the tracing and turn it over. Using a pencil, draw over the outline, covering it thickly. Turn the tracing over again.

3. Lay the tracing on some paper or cardboard. Go over the lines again, so that a line appears on the surface beneath.

4. Remove the tracing paper. You should see the tracing on the new surface. Go over the lines, with a pencil or a ball-point pen.